Breaking
the
Rules

Jennifer Lewis

Breaking the Rules

Jennifer Lewis
Copyright © 2013 by Jennifer Lewis

All Rights Reserved.
Published 2013 by Mangrove
2637 E Atlantic Blvd #24692
Pompano Beach, FL 33062
USA

ISBN: 978-1-939941-03-9

For Bronwyn Jameson
and
Emilie Rose

Many thanks to the generous people who read this book at some point during its creation, including Kathy Altman, Amanda Berry, Carly Carson, Elle Kennedy, Anne MacFarlane, and the multi-talented Lynn Messina.

PROLOGUE

"It's your last night of freedom, Joe. Your choice. You get your future foretold or you get a tattoo."

Joe Figueroa adjusted his white sailor hat and looked from one Second Avenue storefront to another. A neon hand crisscrossed with lines hovered in front of a velvet curtain in the first. A thousand wrinkled, yellowed drawings clung to the glass of the other.

"What happens if I don't want either?"

"Then you'll have to fight me and you don't want to get your pretty white uniform all dirty."

Joe looked at the scrawny pink-faced kid making the threat and laughed. They all wore the same "milkman" uniform that identified them as raw recruits in the Navy.

"Go on Joe, get the tat," called the big kid from Philly.

"Yeah, a well-stacked broad, right there on your chest where you'll appreciate her assets when you're alone in your bunk out on the ocean."

"Nah, Joe's going to get 'mom' tattooed over his heart. He's a momma's boy, you can tell."

"Leave my mom out of this." His words emerged with an unintended edge that spoke of the guilt he felt at leaving her alone. But his dad would have been proud to see him join the Navy. He planned a life that'd make his dad smile down from heaven.

"No way I'm gonna mark up this perfect physique. I'll take my chances with the fortune-teller. Let's see what my grand future has in store for me. You lugs wait out here."

A bell tinkled as he pushed open the heavy steel door and stepped into the darkened space behind the curtain. An unusual aroma filled his nostrils, an exotic incense that made him smile. A taste of the strange and exciting experiences waiting for him on the other side of the world.

As his eyes adjusted to the gloom, he made out a small, round table with a crystal ball sitting all alone on the black velvet cloth. Something brushed against his ankle, and the resulting shot of adrenaline made him flinch.

Just a cat. A black cat.

"Hey, anyone here?" His voice, deep with forced bravado, swirled around him like the scented smoke that curled in the air.

Maybe just a small tattoo on his back...

A door creaked open in the wall behind the table, and a dark-clad figure entered the room.

"Be seated." The soft voice surprised him, feminine, the voice of a young woman. A furtive glance suggested she was about his own age. And pretty.

Joe lowered himself into the wooden chair, hitching up his fitted sailor pants.

"You have three choices."

"Yeah?" Another flash of nervous energy jolted him. She could just look at him and tell he had three choices in life?

"I read your palm for five dollars, I read the tarot

cards for ten dollars, or for fifteen I look into my seeing globe."

"Oh, yeah, right." He wanted to laugh at his own seriousness, but the solemn atmosphere silenced him.

He glanced at the ball sitting on the ornately carved black stand. The orb shimmered in the flickering light from the incense burner, opaque, mysterious, promising a glimpse of the bright future he was eager to begin. "The crystal ball, please."

She held out her hand. Slim, long fingered, pale in the half-light, palm raised toward him. He battled a sudden, unexpected urge to seize it and press his lips into the soft flesh.

"Fifteen dollars, please."

He reached into his pocket and pulled out his billfold, carefully separated the crisp notes, then placed them on her palm. As she curled her fingers around the notes, he looked up into her face. What he saw there made him catch his breath.

Dark eyes shaded by thick lashes fixed him with an inquisitive stare that made his palms tingle. Her lips parted slightly, as if in surprise, and she blinked shyly. The sloe-eyed beauty looked almost as nervous as him.

He pushed a smile to his lips, wanting to set her at ease, wanting to set himself at ease. But she simply looked down at the ball as she slid his money into a fold of her shapeless black garments.

"Can you really see the future in that thing?" He shifted in his chair, trying to diffuse the tension, make some small talk with the pretty fortune-teller.

"Quiet please. I must concentrate." She pressed her lips together. In the dim light they were dark, the color of rosy fall apples, of temptation. Quite a babe, this fortune-teller. Joe settled back in his chair, ready to enjoy the view for a few minutes. Get his fifteen bucks' worth one way or another.

Her straight, shiny black hair hung past her shoulders to where her breasts must be hidden beneath her black top. He wondered what kind of breasts she had. Small and pert, or full and heavy? Were her nipples pale shell pink or dark like the bruise from a love bite?

Ouch. He shifted again. These tight white pants didn't hide much.

She didn't wave her hands around the ball or mutter any incantations the way he might have expected. She simply looked into the milky sphere, eyes keenly focused, face taut with concentration.

Her features were delicate yet strong, proud cheekbones and slightly pointed chin forming a heart shape. The dark fall of hair hid her ears and he wondered if she wore big hoop earrings like a fairground gypsy.

"Are you a gypsy?" He couldn't resist asking as the thought occurred to him. There was something exotic and otherworldly about her that triggered his imagination.

"Yes." She looked up, startled from her intense contemplation. "I am Romani." She stared at him for a moment. "Do you have a problem with that?"

"No." Her sudden hostility surprised him. And intrigued him. "Just curious."

She regarded him for a second, black eyes filled with suspicion, before turning her gaze back to the crystal ball.

Her pursed lips parted for an instant, then snapped shut. A little prick of fear spiked in Joe's gut. Did she see something there that made her hesitate to tell him?

"What?" He cleared his throat.

"Something unexpected."

"Yeah?" He tried to sound casual as he shifted on the uncomfortably hard wooden chair.

"It concerns...*love*." As she said the word *love*, she glanced up at him and pinned him with her haunting gaze for a fraction of a second. Just long enough to suck the breath from his lungs and set his heart pounding.

Her eyes dropped back to the ball, but her rosy lips twitched as if more words danced on her tongue. Her dark lashes flickered, blinking at what she saw.

"Love?" The word felt alien on his tongue, like an unknown word from a foreign language.

His gut tightened as he remembered his dad's words, rasped harshly as the emphysema stole his last breaths: "Love makes a life, son." He hadn't understood it then, and he didn't understand it now, but he'd damn sure try.

He leaned forward, tried to make out something in the milky glass, but saw nothing but his own distorted reflection. A big, raw-boned kid in a goofy sailor getup.

She squinted slightly as she peered into the depths.

Smoky curls of the sweet, heavy incense hung around him, stinging his nostrils, heightening his senses. For the first time he noticed the soft beat of a drum seeping through the walls, pounding a steady rhythm, echoing the elevated beat of his heart.

"Tonight," she intoned softly, lashes flickering over her lowered eyes. "Tonight you will meet the woman you are destined to spend your life with."

1

Ten years later

He had a bone to pick with that fortune-teller. The love of his life? Yeah, the bane of his existence, more like.

Joe strode along Second Avenue, pushing through the happy hour throng gathered on the sidewalks in the hot mid-summer dusk. The sickly-sweet scent of steaming garbage mingled with the smell of hot pierogies, chicken fried rice and raw fish being chopped for sushi.

Home.

It was an odd relief to be back in the city. He'd grown up in Brooklyn and maybe he'd go back there one day, but right now Manhattan, with its teeming crowds of anonymous strangers, was the place for him.

He scanned the storefronts, looking for that neon hand. He'd seen a few of them dotted around the East Village, but he was one hundred percent sure that the one he needed was right here on Second Avenue. He wasn't sure what block, though. Between Ninth and Tenth streets? Nope.

Seventh and Eighth? Fire burned in his gut, along with the two hotdogs-with-everything he'd shoved down there as he wandered the blazing streets. The bulky leather bag slung over his shoulder carried the only possessions he'd bothered to bring with him. Linda could have the rest, along with the house. Material things mattered far more to her than they did to him.

They mattered more to her than he ever had.

Maybe the storefront was gone? Ten years was a long time. Maybe she'd moved or gone out of business or been arrested for fraud? Messing up people's lives with phony predictions should come with a stiff penalty.

He should have gone with the tattoo. He had more than one now anyway. And recently had one very painfully removed. The raw patch of skin still itched and burned.

A flash across the street caught his eye. Sun glinting off glass, momentarily obscuring the familiar curves of neon tubing shaped into an outward-facing hand.

Stop! That was what the hand said to him now. If only he'd had that reaction ten years ago.

A fresh flush of anger goaded him across the street. He strode through honking traffic right up to the scuffed metal door leading into the storefront.

He hesitated for a second, steadying himself, hand on the worn brass knob.

He'd been to hell and back and had the scars to prove it—inside and out. He'd stared death in the face and survived the death of his dreams. What was he doing here? Did he really think scolding some phony fortune-teller would make him feel better?

He didn't know what the hell he was doing any more, and it scared him. He was just trying to put one foot in front of the other and keep on keeping on. With that thought, he pushed hard on the heavy door and stepped blindly into the smoky darkness behind it.

The rich, heavy incense stung his eyes as he waited for his vision to penetrate the dim atmosphere. The table was there, velvet cloth hanging to the floor, with the big glass ball glowing ominously in the shimmering light from the incense burner. The wood chair still stood in front of it, waiting to support the squirming backsides of gullible strangers.

He saw the outline of the door in the dark wall behind the table. Suddenly it cracked open an inch. Joe threw his shoulders back, clenched his gut as if anticipating a hard fist.

"You have three choices."

"I know."

Susana pushed out into the room, stifling a yawn. The man's brusque response made her lift her eyes to get a look at him. From his response he sounded like a regular, but she didn't recognize him.

Or maybe she did.

She narrowed her eyes, squinting through the smoke. Something oddly familiar about him sent a shiver along her vertebrae. His hardness jolted her: rigid posture, taut muscles, his hostile stare.

And those eyes.

Black in the darkness, his eyes spoke of pain that sent a sharp echo ringing through her. A pain strong enough to sap the life force of a man. To suck the energy out of those around him. A sorrow that feeds and grows, like a living thing.

She suppressed a shudder.

She'd seen more than her fair share of sad eyes. Hurt eyes, haunted eyes, desperate, bitter, lonely eyes. People didn't come to a fortune-teller when their life was going the way they wanted. They came when they needed help.

"I read your palm for five dollars..."

"I'm not here for a reading." He spat out the words, cutting her off.

Again she was struck by the odd sense of familiarity. Something about the cut of his jaw, the shape of his skull beneath the cropped dark hair, something about those eyes...

"Why are you here?" Curiosity swelled inside her like the opening notes of an unfamiliar tune.

"To see you."

The force with which he spoke made her hold her breath.

Let him speak. He has something to say.

She watched him, caution stinging her fingers and toes. She wasn't naïve about the dangers of her profession. Alone in a darkened storefront with one troubled, needy stranger after another.

But she had the strength of her ancestors to guide and protect her. Their wisdom and otherworldly knowledge flowed in her blood. She walked among people, yet apart from them, separated from them by mysteries she could never explain.

"Are you some kind of witch?"

"No!" She bit back the indignation that surged at his accusation. The days of her kind being burned at the stake were over, at least for now.

"I asked because you don't look a single day older." He tilted his head, facing her in suspicious half-profile. "I was here ten years ago. Ten long years that are etched all over my face, and you look exactly the same." His face was contorted with confusion, his handsome features tight with worry.

"Ten years ago my grandmother would have given

the reading."

"No." He shook his head, his dark stare so fierce it threatened to knock her off her feet. "No, it was you. You read my future in the crystal ball." His eyes darted to the sphere and back to hers. "Right here. While I sat in that chair you told me I would meet the love of my life that very night."

The bile in his words audibly choked him, and for a second she longed to reach out and offer the simple consolation of a touch. But she'd been warned against the dangers of stepping outside the bounds.

She did know him, though. Susana narrowed her eyes again as the memory of that night formed in her mind's eye.

"It was you," he said, his words a harsh indictment.

"It was me," she replied softly. "It was the first reading I ever did."

"Your first reading?" Aggression twisted his lip. "So you were just making stuff up off the top of your head? How old were you anyway?"

"I was thirteen."

"Jesus." Shock flickered in his eyes.

"I was young, but I had experience working with the seeing globe. My grandmother taught me everything she knew."

A familiar pang of sorrow accompanied the thought of her beloved Granna. Her own skills had now surpassed the older woman's. Susana's psychic abilities were stronger, her gift for intuitive readings deeper and more subtle. But she still missed Granna's supportive strength and reassuring confidence every day.

"So she taught you to make a sucker cross your palm with silver, then scheme up something to get him running out the door with a smile on his face?" His hard eyes bored into her as he stood there, fists clenched, spitting his arrows of accusation.

She held her tongue. *It's the hurt talking*. Something terrible had happened to him.

Pity stirred in her heart along with something else. Something deeper, sharper. Something invigorating and alarming.

She remembered that first reading as clearly as if she'd seen it in the globe that morning. Two lovers. The fresh-faced young boy he'd been that night, glowing with hopeful optimism and lust for a life he'd barely begun. And a girl.

But not just any girl.

A black haired girl with cat's eyes and a heart shaped face. A girl who stood in shadow, seeing things no one else could see.

Her.

She'd seen them together in the globe that night. Eyeing each other tentatively. Reaching out a careful hand. Joining those hands and walking together. A slim solemn gypsy girl and the broad shouldered *gadjo* boy who'd sat in front of her.

And she'd never breathed a word of it to anyone.

It had been her first reading for a stranger. She was a young girl, her visions unreliable. Or so she thought.

Now she knew better.

"I told you the truth about what I saw." Fear tightened her throat.

"You saw me meeting the love of my life that night." Filled with pain, his eyes searched her face.

Did he want to think she'd been lying? That she'd lie to him now?

Would she? His heavy burden of sorrow and anger frightened her. He was no longer the innocent boy she'd met all those years ago.

A few dismissive words would make him go away, and she doubted she'd see him again.

"I did see you meeting the love of your life that night."

"But she wasn't. I thought she was..." A muscle twitched in his cheek. "I thought she loved me." His voice cracked and Susana's heart clutched in response.

"I said you would meet the love of your life. But I didn't tell you who she was. I didn't describe the woman I saw in the seeing globe that evening."

She glanced at the globe as icy fingers of apprehension clawed at her gut.

Should she tell him?

"No, that's true." His expression softened a little. "You didn't describe her." His fists still hung clenched at his sides. His plain white T-shirt stretched over his muscled chest, revealing the raw physical strength coiled and waiting in his hard body.

All that strength scared her.

"Was she blonde?" He spoke hesitantly, suspicion darkening his eyes. "The woman you saw?"

She shook her head.

"What did she look like?" A wary look flickered over his strong features. He didn't trust her, but he was listening.

She held her head steady, held his gaze as she spoke. "She looked like me."

He blinked and flinched very slightly. "You?"

"I saw myself in the globe when I did your reading that night."

There. She'd said it. She stiffened, bracing against any number of possible reactions: rage, disgust, disbelief, violent retribution.

But he looked curious. His broad shoulders shifted a little, as if he could rearrange the heavy burden they carried.

"Why didn't you say so?"

She shrugged, trying to lighten her own burden of responsibility, the obligation she'd shirked when she told him only half the reading. "I was young. I didn't have faith in my ability to read accurately. I thought perhaps I was seeing what I wished to see."

"You wished to see yourself—with me?"

"Perhaps."

What thirteen-year-old girl didn't dream of walking arm in arm with a handsome boy? A carefree, healthy young man in a white sailor suit. He'd been the stuff of teenage fantasies back then, with his dark hair buzzed short, his handsome face shaved clean and his dark eyes shining with youthful optimism.

Different from the man who stood before her now. The man whose lips parted as he struggled for words. The youthful optimism gone, replaced by a hard stare of accusation leveled at the world and at her in particular. His striking features marred by a semicircular scar that pierced one eyebrow, and the dark stubble shadowed under his jutting cheekbones.

"Thirteen years old!" He shook his head. "And I listened to you as if you were the Oracle at Delphi. Don't know why I did. I came into the storefront on a dare. I guess you told me what I wanted to hear, so I chose to believe it."

"You wanted to find love?" She spoke so softly her words almost disappeared in the smoke from the incense burner.

"Yeah." He nodded. "Who doesn't?"

"Do you still want to find love?" The words slipped

out of her mouth before she had a chance to catch them. What was she doing?

His reply was a dismissive snort. "No, no, no. I'm all done with *love*. No more for me, thanks." He shook his head again, and a bitter, silent laugh racked him. "Love, hate and everything in between. I'm done with it. I'm not going to marry anybody or fight anybody ever again."

The glint of dark humor in his eyes surprised her. Susana struggled to keep her confusion from showing on her face.

"Funny thought, isn't it?" He let out a sharp choke of laughter. "I had the hots for you that night. While you were sitting there reading my fortune, I was thinking about your breasts."

Her breasts stirred under her black T-shirt as his eyes boldly dropped to survey them.

"I'm thinking about them right now. Guess I don't have any shame left any more."

Susana swallowed hard, trying to shove down the very unfamiliar sensation building underneath her baggy shirt, sliding hotly down into her long, black skirt.

He glanced up and raised his eyebrows. "Do I disgust you?"

"No." She shook her head. She didn't know what she was feeling, but disgust didn't play any part in it.

"I should have disgusted you back then. A big, horny twenty-year old boy eyeing a thirteen-year-old girl. Sounds like a recipe for disaster." Bitter humor flashed in his eyes again. "Then again, maybe a jail term would have saved me some of the other trouble I had instead."

His eyes fell to her breasts again. Her nipples tightened, heating under his gaze.

"What would you have said if I'd asked you out that

night?"

"I'd have had to say no."

"Why?"

"I was engaged to be married."

"At thirteen?" His expression of shocked surprise almost made her smile.

"It's not unusual among my people."

"So you're married?" His forehead creased as he asked the question.

"No." She shook her head. "The engagement was cancelled. My grandmother needed me to stay with her, to develop my gifts."

"And I was the lucky man you tried them out on for the first time." He nodded grimly, a smile struggling to break across his lips. His body still taut, emotion and motion reined tightly as he watched her.

"It wasn't planned." She shrugged, again trying to absolve herself of the growing sense of responsibility gnawing at her. "My grandmother was smoking a cigarette out back. She told me to step in for her."

"You were nervous, weren't you?"

"A little."

"I could see that. It made me like you. Made me see you as a person. Now I can see it should have made me nervous too."

One fist unclenched, and he rubbed a spot on his chest with the extended fingers. The action pulled his thin, white T-shirt tight across the thick curve of his pec, and again Susana's body responded with an alarming flare of heat.

"You were anxious, too." A smile flickered across her lips at the memory of the strapping young man in his white sailor suit, shifting from foot to foot, waiting for her to emerge through the door.

"Yeah? I guess most people are when they're about to hear what the future has in store."

"Only if they plan to believe what they hear."

"Like I said, I just came in on a dare. I sat in that chair"—he gestured toward it—"and I wondered about your breasts." Again his eyes flicked over them, and goose bumps rose over the swollen flesh. Susana tossed her head, lifting her chin, defying her body to respond to his crude gawking.

"You misinterpreted the information I gave you."

"You withheld the information I needed."

He fixed her with his hard stare again, dark eyes holding hers as if a beam of black light shot between them. She faltered, wilting under the heat of his gaze.

He was right. She had cheated him. Committed a sin of omission.

"I'm sorry."

"You're sorry? Yeah? Well, I'm sorry, too." He paused, unclenched his fists and settled his hands on his hips. The gesture enlarged him visually until he seemed to fill the entire space of the small storefront. "And I think you owe me."

He hissed the words quietly, and they slid into Susana's ears, ruffling her nerves, undermining her carefully cultivated professional demeanor.

"I owe you another reading?" She shivered. She didn't want to do a reading for him now. Changed as he was, twisted and tormented by circumstance, she was afraid of what she'd see.

Especially since his future had once been bound up with hers.

"Hell, no. No more readings." He held his head high, dark eyes unreadable in the smoky gloom. "You owe me my life back."

"Only you can shape your own life." The words emerged with a quiver of apprehension. People always wanted more than she could give. She could only read the future, not make it happen. And fate was not a hard, immutable thing, but a frame of possibilities, constantly shifting, changing, as destiny and circumstance writhed together in their unscripted dance.

"You owe me one night, then." His low voice rumbled through the smoke and darkness, setting off a vibration that echoed deep inside her.

"No." She choked the word, hands fisting into her skirt. Smoking trails of heat simmered through her body where his eyes danced over her.

"An evening. Dinner." He tilted his head slightly, thoughtfully, as if contemplating an unfolding scroll of possibilities. That bitter laugh shook him. "Dinner and a movie, just like regular folks."

"It's not a good idea." Nerves all on edge, she resisted the urge to shrink away from him. Her nipples strained against the fabric of her shirt. Her fingertips hummed with unwelcome anticipation as she buried them in the folds of her skirt and struggled to stay totally still. To resist his power.

"I don't care if it's a good idea. I did everything right and look where I am now. A bad idea is as good as any, as far as I'm concerned. Are you afraid of me?"

Yes.

"No."

"Then why not? You've got to eat. I'll buy you a good dinner. I've got to eat, too. I guess that's one thing we have in common."

Her nerves shrieked an alarm of warning. But woven through the wail of fear was an opposite call—a siren song bidding her to taste the dangerous and forbidden fruit of dinner with the handsome boy she'd seen in her globe so long ago.

To taste the freedom she craved.

She consulted her sixth sense—her bread and butter, the precious gift she'd cultivated until it was stronger than her other senses.

Silence and darkness. No answers forthcoming.

"Come on." He reached out a hand. Her eyes fell to the thick muscles of his forearm, the tan skin sprinkled with tiny dark hairs. Warm human flesh reaching out to her.

"Okay."

2

The rumble of the corrugated metal awning shuddered through Susana's body. It clanged to the ground with grim finality. She pulled the key out of the padlock with an ominous sense that she was leaving behind the safe little world she inhabited and stepping out into a fearsome new universe of possibility.

She tucked the key into her pocket.

Joe stood there, features thrown into relief by the harsh glare of the streetlights, hands shoved in his pockets, oblivious to the strangers pushing past him.

"Ready?"

She nodded. And swallowed. She'd never been to dinner with any man other than her cousins Janus and Roman. If they knew she was about to have dinner with a complete stranger—worse, a *gadjo*...

They'd better not find out.

She tucked a lock of hair behind her ear.

"Where do you want to go?" Joe offered her his arm. The gesture startled her—formal, and yet so intimate. An invitation to touch him right there in the street. She lifted her elbow and cautiously threaded her arm though his.

Tiny hairs stood on end, mingling as the crooks of

their elbows intertwined. Susana struggled to keep her breathing shallow as the odd sensation of touching a man heated her blood and quickened her pulse.

"Indian?" He turned his head to her. "We could go to Sixth Street. What kind of food do you like?"

"Indian food sounds good." It sounded good partly because her cousins disliked spicy food so she was unlikely to run into them there.

And partly because she liked it.

"Let's go." He flashed her a quick smile, and she instinctively smiled back. *Weird*. They set off walking at a slow pace, arm in arm.

Her long skirt rustled about her legs and she wished she were wearing jeans. Granna always said fortune-tellers should dress the way people expected, as it inspired confidence. She'd prefer to have the accuracy of her predictions inspire confidence, but she knew better than to defy Granna.

What on earth would Granna think of her accepting a stranger's invitation to dinner? Or walking arm in arm with him down a public street?

She caught her breath at the thought.

"You okay?"

"Of course." She forced a quick smile. Granna was gone. She was on her own now and could make her own decisions.

Shape her own destiny.

She sneaked a glance at the tall man beside her. Head held high, chin jutting defiantly, Joe walked as if he owned the sidewalk.

He had little in common with the fresh-faced boy who'd walked into the store ten years earlier. Time and circumstance had made his features bolder and his physique broader. The fine lines that etched his skin spoke of time spent under an unforgiving sun and the deepening of unique character traits.

She felt a little flush of pride at walking arm in arm with such an attractive man. And a frisson of apprehension. Her old prediction had come true. He'd reached out to her and she'd taken his hand—his arm.

She didn't know what came next. At the time she hadn't wanted to see. She'd been scared of the forbidden and dangerous vision that flickered in the globe. Scared of her own powers, so new and barely harnessed. Scared of Granna, too.

Shocked and frightened, she'd wrapped up the reading and ushered him out of the store as quickly as she could.

But he'd come back.

"I don't know your name," she said with as much normalcy as she could muster.

"Joe." He turned to her. "Joe Figueroa. And yours?"

"Susana Cigan."

He'd seen her looking furtively about as they walked along the sidewalk, shying from the stray glances of strangers, as if she didn't want to be seen in public with him.

No sweat. He didn't want to be seen in public with himself, either. If disappearing into thin air could be done, he'd have tried it.

Since he was still here, however, he had to eat. Why not look at a pretty girl while he did it?

Susana lowered herself into a chair and arranged her long skirt around her legs. She shot him a shy smile. Like a girl on a date. Cute.

Had he asked a girl out on a damn date? A witchy fortune-teller broad, no less? He was crazy all right, no doubt about that. But he couldn't deny that, right now, the evening shimmered with all kinds of intriguing promise.

A waiter handed them menus and he eased himself back in his chair. Susana opened her menu and studied it intently, lashes lowered and lips slightly parted.

She was definitely a babe. Speaking of which...

"So if you were thirteen back then, you're twenty-three now."

She glanced up, startled. "Yes."

"You tell fortunes for a living?"

"Yes. I used to work with my grandmother and I took over her business when she died."

"I don't imagine it pays too well."

"I need little money to live."

Joe remembered the check in his pocket. A simple piece of folded paper worth nearly two million dollars.

"Rent controlled apartment, huh?"

"Yes." She smiled slightly, revealing even rows of small white teeth. Everything about her was small and delicate. Except her hair. Thick and jet black, it fell in a gleaming sheet over her narrow shoulders.

"So you've worked in that storefront since you were thirteen?"

She nodded.

"Didn't you ever want to do anything else?"

Susana blinked, her lashes so thick that her eyes appeared to be ringed by dark kohl. "It's my life's work to read fortunes."

"Is that what your grandmother told you?"

"My grandmother was a very wise woman."

"And I'll bet she ruled you with an iron fist."

"She didn't have to. I've always been obedient." She flashed a defiant glance at him, and he saw a spark of the fire that simmered beneath her calm surface.

That fire excited him. He could feel its heat even as she maintained her cool composure.

Are you a virgin?

The question hummed on his lips but remained unspoken.

"You've always done what your family wanted?"

"Yes." She picked up her glass and sipped her water, avoiding his glance.

"But they wouldn't want you to be here with me now, would they?"

What was he doing? Trying to scare her off? Drive her away?

Maybe.

"No." She answered quickly, holding his gaze.

"And why are you?"

"Because you asked me." She said it simply, looking suddenly shy. On impulse he reached across the table, palm up, inviting her to take his hand.

But she didn't. She glanced at it, then up at him, and quickly back to her menu.

He withdrew his hand.

"What about your parents—where are they?"

"My parents are dead." She fixed him with a stony gaze that dared him to ask more. That warned him against it.

He didn't have the energy for anyone else's sob story right now. "Mine, too."

"I'm sorry."

"You're sorry about a lot of things, aren't you?"

She picked up her glass and took a hesitant sip, as if the liquid in it might be neat gin.

"What do you want from me?" Her voice trembled slightly as she put her glass down, careful not to spill water on the white tablecloth.

"I don't know. I don't know what I want any more. Except maybe tandoori chicken, aloo paratha and cucumber raita."

A smile twitched at the corner of her mouth. "That's a start."

The waiter took their orders as costumed musicians climbed onto a tiny stage.

One man began tapping on a traditional drum, and the rhythm pounded through the small restaurant. Susana broke off a small piece of poppadum and placed it on her tongue.

"Spicy?"

She swallowed it. "A little."

He watched her long, elegant fingers as she broke off another morsel.

"Will you feed some to me?"

She glanced up at him, regarded him warily. Then, with a deadly serious expression, she snapped off a fragment and extended it toward his mouth. Silver bracelets slid down her slim wrist, clanging together as she reached toward him.

He parted his lips, surprised. He'd expected nothing more than a charming rejection. She placed the morsel right on his tongue, like a priest offering communion, holding his gaze while she did it.

The pepper stung his tongue as arousal fired his body.

She withdrew her arm, bracelets sliding back down as she broke off another piece for herself. Cool and calm, as if she fed a starving, desperate man every day of her life.

And maybe she did. Feeding people tidbits of hope, tantalizing fragments of cherished dreams.

"Do people usually have a specific question when they come for a reading?"

"Often they do."

"I bet they have an answer they want, too."

"No doubt you're right." She paused, brushing crumbs from her slim fingers.

"I guess that was my problem the day I showed up in your store. Even though it wasn't my idea. I wanted to hear that everything was going to work out just the way I planned it. Happy ever after, you know."

"I suppose that's what everyone wants."

"You too?"

"Me?"

"You're human aren't you?"

She didn't answer. Maybe she considered herself above the joys and troubles of ordinary mortals. She picked up her glass and took another sip, her solemn expression unreadable. Her lips the color of a bruise as they closed over the hard rim of her glass.

She wasn't like other people. She could see the future and choose whether to share her knowledge or keep it to herself.

The waiter served their food. Susana ate slowly, hesitantly, tasting each mouthful with painstaking deliberation. Joe suspected she approached everything in her life with such cool calculation. Did she ever lose control?

He reached for a piece of paratha and at the same moment she reached too. Her fingertips brushed the back of his hand, short nails grazing the skin.

She jerked her hand back as if he'd stung it. "Sorry."

She blinked. Nervous. His skin buzzed a little where she'd touched it, stray electrical impulses remaining even after she'd withdrawn her hand.

"Here." He handed her a piece of bread and she took it hesitantly.

"Thank you." She lowered her eyes as she ripped the soft paratha with delicate movements of her hands, bracelets clinking.

As she opened her mouth, he wondered what it would be like to push his tongue between those slim lips and taste the mysteries within.

Was that a vision of the future?

Or the mental wanderings of a desperate man?

He shoved a big forkful of chicken in his mouth and washed it down with a gulp of water. Shoved some bread in, too. Suddenly he was ravenous and had to keep reminding himself not to gulp down his food as if he were back in the mess hall.

The exotic aromas heightened his senses, his tongue alive with the taste of the spices.

On the stage the musicians had finished warming up and tuning their instruments, and now played with vigor. The sharp singing notes of the sitar rang through the air like the voice of a mournful woman.

Joe glanced up at Susana and wasn't the slightest bit surprised to see her watching him. Reading him.

"What do you see?" His question sounded like the challenge it was.

"A man." She held his gaze.

"What kind of man?" His gut tightened. How did he look to a stranger? He'd been afraid of mirrors lately. Not wanting to see his empty eyes.

"A sad one." She said it softly, almost apologetic.

The haunting minor scale notes of the unfamiliar music swept through her words and turned them into a song.

"Is there a gypsy cure for sadness?" He tried to make

light of it.

A smile flickered across her lips. "Yes."

"Oh yeah?" A spark of adrenaline kicked in his gut. "Can you heal me?"

"Only if you want to be healed. If you're ready to leave your sadness behind."

Again the music wove through her voice, transforming her soft speech into a melodic chant. The effect was a little hypnotic. Joe struggled to keep his wits about him.

"Who wouldn't?"

She surveyed him coolly. "Sadness can be a protective cloak. An armor that shields you from further pain." She paused, her penetrating black gaze unsettling. "I think you know that."

"I don't think I know much of anything any more."

He could see the pulse in her slim neck, and he tried to distract himself with thoughts of how that fluttering heartbeat might feel under his lips.

But already memories were crowding his consciousness. Memories that trailed after him, clanking against the guilt in a ball and chain of mistakes and failures that would drag behind him the rest of his life.

Memories of that one night that was the beginning of the end.

The drumming quickened, rising to a crescendo as the wailing song of the sitar filled his ears like a scream of panic. Panic that ripped through his nerves.

"Let's get out of here." He leapt to his feet, shoving his chair clumsily against the patron behind him. "Sorry." He groped in his pocket for change. A $50 was the smallest thing he had so he threw it on the table and grabbed his bag.

Confusion covered Susana's face as she rose slowly

from her chair. He grabbed her hand where it paused on the table. Seized it in his and pulled her. He needed to get outside, breathe the night air. And he needed her with him.

He stumbled out into the hot, dark night, gasping for breath as the high-pitched keening of the sitar pursued him like his nightmares. He clutched her small hand, its coolness a balm to him.

"Where are we going?" Her voice a little breathless, her eyes wide, she struggled to keep up with him as he strode down Sixth Street.

"To the water."

Water calmed him. The endless flow, the powerful streaming persistence of it. Nothing could stop water. Dams, doors, banks, cliffs, canyons—sooner or later they all gave way under the heavy weight, the relentless pressure. The heaving presence of an unbreakable life force.

He headed for the East River because it was closer. Susana followed him, quickening her pace to keep up with him and soon they were both running. The night air filled his lungs, soothing the restlessness that assaulted him if he stayed still too long. His blood pumped from exertion, not anxiety, and his brain calmed.

He glanced sideways at Susana as she ran beside him, her long skirt clutched in one hand and her face lit with a breathless smile. He caught her eye and she laughed, a carefree burst that thrilled his heart to hear it.

They shoved and jostled their way past the scattered crowds, breaking their pace only to weave through a honking stream of cars. Traffic roared beneath them as they took the footbridge over the highway, descending at last into the cool, dark stillness of East River Park.

"Isn't it dangerous, coming to the park this late?" Susana gasped the words, still running, her hand hot in his.

"Anything can be dangerous."

But she didn't look worried. Her face glowed as they pounded across tarmac and grass toward the beckoning dark swell of the river.

At the embankment they stopped, and Joe dropped his bag and steadied himself with a hand on the cool hard stone. He turned to Susana and she bent over, gasping for breath, laughter escaping her in panting bursts.

"What are we doing here?" she gasped, her smiling mouth half hidden by windblown black hair. Her golden skin shone under the nearby streetlight, and her lips and cheeks flushed dark.

"I guess we'll find out when it happens."

Already this was the craziest, most exciting night of her life. Her heart thundered at the unaccustomed exertion, the rousing unpredictability.

Joe still held her hand tight, their hot fingers intertwined. His pulse mingled with hers in a fierce primal tune.

"Look at the water," he said, wonder in his voice.

"It's so black." She shuddered a little at the heaving, night-colored mass.

"It's beautiful, ruthless, it never gives up." He turned to face her, his bold features etched in moonlight. "It seeps in through cracks, trickles down crevices, drips and flows, pours and rushes." Laughter sparkled in his eyes. "It always gets where it's going."

A laugh bubbled up inside her. An echoing response to his unexpected boyish exuberance. The sound pealed out into the night air and sparked a grin that cracked across Joe's face.

The clean tang of his sweat caught her by surprise, mingled with the reassuring scent of detergent and soap, the smell of a healthy male. He suddenly seemed so alive, so vigorous.

But she knew that other man lurked beneath the surface. The hard bitter man who'd come into her *ofisa* demanding answers, seeking retribution.

A little shiver of fear crept up her spine as she realized she was all alone in a darkened park with that man. Any screams would be lost in the roar of traffic on FDR Drive, which separated the park from the rest of the city.

She tossed her head, wild strands of hair dancing in front of her eyes. She'd never taken a chance like this. Never done something so blatantly foolish. Never done anything so irresistibly thrilling.

"Susana."

"Yes." Her voice emerged as a scared whisper.

"Do you believe in fate?"

"Yes."

"Do you believe that perhaps..." He paused, glanced out at the heaving black water. Her breath caught in her throat as she waited for him to finish.

But he didn't.

Instead he pulled her to him with one quick motion, wrapped his free arm around her back and settled his hot mouth over hers.

His tongue pried her lips open and probed into her mouth. An instinctive adrenaline rush of resistance stung her, urging her to fight back. But she didn't.

A blistering swell of heat rose through her, starting deep in her belly and seeping along her limbs until her fingers and toes sizzled.

You're kissing a man.

The taste of forbidden fruit burned her tongue, exciting in its punishing spiciness.

Joe's hands slid along her back, pulling her closer until her breasts sank against his hard chest. Calloused fingers danced along her spine, teasing the flesh through her thin shirt, sparking trails of heat that shimmered under his touch.

Her nipples tightened against his firm muscle, thrilling to the hard masculinity of his body.

Who are you, Joe Figueroa? Who was this man she'd seen so long ago—his fate entwined with hers? A vision so strange it made her doubt the strength of her own gifts.

Right now her body didn't care who he was. Didn't care about fate, destiny or the future that lay even five minutes away.

Joe licked the inside of her upper lip, triggering a gasp as the sensitive nerve endings shivered under his touch. Then he plunged deep into her mouth.

His tongue wound around hers as his arms pulled her close, drawing their bodies tighter and tighter in an unforgiving embrace.

And she found herself kissing him back.

With her teeth she grazed his tongue, tested his lower lip. Her mouth teased over his hard cheekbone as she strained upward on tiptoes, wanting to claim his face with her mouth.

Joe bent down to give her the access she craved. Her heart stirred at his trust when she brushed her lips over his eyelids, feeling his eyeballs flicker beneath them.

She skimmed her lips over the semicircle of his scar, tracing the slight indentation with her tongue, and sensed him shudder slightly as she did.

His breath burned hot on her neck, his lips on her pulse as she explored him, trailing her mouth over the sharp prickle of his unshaved cheeks. The roughness of his face stung her swollen lips, exciting in its unfamiliar maleness.

Curls of desire rose though her like smoke, creeping along her limbs and making them heavy. Joe's thick arms supported her, holding her close and tight as she allowed the sensation to flood her.

His mouth tickled her ear, hot breath sparking a little tremor as he whispered, "I don't believe in fate."

Her eyes flashed open, falling on the half moon shivering in the silent black water. Then his eyes caught hers, black and unreadable, and a quiver of alarm rang through her.

"What do you believe in?" Her voice emerged reedy and breathless, hung with apprehension.

"Life. Clinging to life with everything you've got."

She could see the hardness in him then, its brittle bitterness gleaming beneath the surface of his skin. And she could see it now for what it was—his life force, an unbreakable diamond forged in the furnace of whatever he'd been through.

She shuddered gently, afraid of his past. Afraid of her own future.

Joe rubbed her back softly. "Cold?"

"A little."

A night breeze dispersed the blistering heat and humidity of the day. Its cool breath on her skin soothed her, taming the fierce inferno of desire Joe had triggered with his shocking kiss.

It wasn't the cold that caused her tremors, but she didn't want him to know that.

He pulled his arms gently away from her and she shivered again, suddenly bereft of his warm touch.

He bent down and unzipped his bag, fished around in it, then brought out a dark sweatshirt.

"Here." He arranged it carefully over her shoulders.

His thumb touched her chin tentatively, and he looked into her eyes. "Maybe we shouldn't be out here in the middle of the night." The wary expression in his eyes seemed almost shy. "Sometimes I get these crazy urges. I've learned to act on them."

"I'm glad you did." The words slipped out before she could stop them. Her lips still stung with the force of his kiss, her belly tight with the heat coiling inside it.

"Me too."

His eyes gleamed with something that shone through the hardness, a vital warmth she saw there for the first time. Had their kiss lit a flame inside him, too?

A moment of awkwardness followed. Now that they weren't touching each other a gulf suddenly gaped between them.

"I need to find a hotel room before it gets too late."

"You don't live in the city?"

"Nope. Not yet anyway. I arrived this morning from western PA."

"Oh."

"You wondering where my luggage is?"

She shook her head. He didn't seem like a man who'd have luggage. Just baggage.

"Well, in case you are and you're too polite to ask, I don't have any. I'm a rolling stone. Wherever I hang my hat, that's my home." He winked at her.

A smile teased across her lips. "You don't have a hat."

"Nope, and I don't plan to get one either. Too much stuff just weighs you down."

Stuff. She knew all about that. She lived surrounded by decades' accumulation of someone else's stuff. The old furniture, the old rugs, the old knickknacks.

The old ways.

A sudden vision of Joe standing in her grandmother's apartment tickled the beginnings of a giggle inside her.

Her grandmother's apartment? It was her apartment now.

Her grandmother was gone. Though she did live on in all the dust-gathering clutter she'd left behind. And in all the rules and codes and warnings and arcane rituals she'd left behind to clutter Susana's mind.

The thought of Joe's big, brawny, untidy, rather hostile presence in the midst of her grandmother's lace-festooned parlor suddenly seemed irresistibly appealing.

The suppressed chuckle burst up and became a laugh.

"What's so funny?" His brow wrinkled with confusion even as a smile tugged at the corners of his mouth.

"I just had a crazy thought."

"Yeah?" He raised an eyebrow.

Susana bit her lip. Was she really about to ask a man back to her apartment? A man who'd just stolen her breath with an uninvited kiss?

It was a terrible idea.

"You were in the Navy, weren't you?"

A terrible idea that made her toes tingle with excitement.

"Yes." Joe tipped his head, curious. "Seven years."

"So you know how to obey rules."

Joe pursed his lips and nodded his head. "I guess I have some practice with that."

"And you need a place to sleep?"

"Sure do."

She hesitated and he waited quietly, watching her. Expectation hummed in the air between them.

"I live a few blocks from here, near Delancey Street."

"Oh?"

She could see wheels turning in Joe's head, but he kept quiet. Waiting for her to make her move.

"And if you can agree to a few ground rules..." She lifted her chin. "If you can commit to those rules..." She stared hard at him, defying him to lie to her. "Then you could come stay overnight. If you like."

As she said the last words it suddenly occurred to her that he might not want to.

But a hotel room would cost him upwards of $100 and she didn't think he had that kind of change burning a hole in his pocket.

He didn't reply right away though.

Joe's eyes narrowed and he surveyed her coolly.

"And what exactly would these rules be?"

She tossed her head and drew his sweatshirt about her.

"No touching."

"No touching." He nodded thoughtfully, surveying her with suspicious black eyes. "And? You said 'rules.' That's just one."

"No poking about."

He raised an eyebrow. "I'd think no touching pretty much ruled out poking."

"I mean through her possessions."

"Whose possessions?"

"My grandmother."

"Your grandmother lives there, too?"

"She used to."

If Granna was still in residence there would be *no way* Joe could set foot in that apartment. Not and live to tell the tale, anyway.

"She died?"

"Six months ago."

"I'm sorry."

"Me, too." And she was. Her grandmother had raised her, been a mother to her after her own mother died so suddenly.

But another part of her was glad to be free.

Free to do something crazy, something stupid, something dangerous and maybe wonderful.

"So you live alone?" Joe hoisted his bag onto his shoulder.

A prickle of fear raised the hairs on her neck.

"Yes," she murmured hesitantly. "I live alone."

Spoken aloud it made her sound vulnerable. Easy prey.

"I'll obey the rules. Heck, it'll be nice to be in a home and not some dumpy hotel room. I've stayed in enough of those lately. I'll keep my hands to myself."

He shoved the hands in question deep into the pockets of his faded jeans. "See?"

Susana chuckled, tamping down the swell of apprehension that stirred in her chest as they set off back toward the city streets.

She knew she had good instincts about people. She'd honed them over the last ten years of prying into strangers' lives. She had a good feeling about Joe. He needed help, no doubt about that. Could she help him? Maybe, maybe not.

Did she trust him? Kind of. She trusted him probably as much as he trusted himself.

And for now, that was enough.

3

"Jesus."

Still breathless from the climb up six flights of stairs, Joe was unprepared for the strange world that awaited him on the other side of the battered door to Susana's apartment.

Her grandmother's apartment.

For the old lady clearly still resided there in spirit, if not in body.

Every surface in the apartment was crowded and cluttered with things. Boxes, candlesticks, icons, vases, trinkets of every size and description.

Heavy lace covered the windows and ancient floral wallpaper peeked out from behind the many pictures hung on the walls or simply stuck on with tape. Susana stood against the far wall, her back stiff, her eyes darting first around the room and then to him.

"It's not a big place," she started apologetically.

Joe cut her off. "It might be if it didn't have so much stuff in it. I thought gypsies were supposed to travel light?"

"I guess this is what happens when they stay put too long." A nervous smile played about her lips. "I never could get her to part with anything."

She glanced around the room and a tremor of sadness passed over her features. "She came here from Europe in the 1940s. She'd been imprisoned by the Nazis. She had nothing and all her family was dead."

"Jesus." Joe raked a hand through his hair.

"This was her refuge from a world she didn't trust. I guess she piled up all this stuff around her as protection, to keep her from having nothing, from being no one again."

Joe blew out a blast of air. The cloying atmosphere in the room threatened to suck the breath from his body.

"She raised her family here. She had three children. And she raised me."

"And now you can't bring yourself to dismantle the world she created."

"Oh, I'm sure I will eventually." She removed his sweatshirt from her shoulders and folded it up. The apartment was warm, oppressively so.

She set it down on a chair and smoothed a hand over her T-shirt, tucking it tighter into the waistband of her long skirt.

Joe's breath hitched as the action pulled the stretchy fabric tight against her breasts. Uh-oh, there he went, thinking about her breasts again. He was beginning to suspect they were on the large side. With no bra restraining them.

He shifted as his jeans tightened. *Remember the rules.*

He respected her rules. This was her home, her sanctuary. They barely knew each other.

But damn she'd felt good in his arms.

The tiny hairs on his arms pricked up at the memory. Susana held tight in his embrace, warm and soft, all woman.

He'd kissed her on impulse, an irresistible urge to

taste her berry-colored lips. He'd lost track of his own rules. He was surviving on impulse now.

And he didn't regret acting on it. He'd kissed her, and she'd kissed him back with a heat that threatened to engulf his own.

"Can I offer you some tea?" Her rather formal request clashed with his steamy thoughts and startled him.

She tucked a lock of hair nervously behind her ear.

"Uh, sure." Maybe tea would help calm the fever that raged in his blood as he remembered the hot, sweet taste of her mouth.

Are you a virgin?

The question remained unanswered. His eyes tracked Susana as she slid into the tiny kitchen, disappearing from view.

There couldn't be too many twenty-three-year-old virgins left in New York City.

But then there weren't many twenty-three-year-old gypsy fortune-tellers who lived with their grandma either. Sure, the old woman had been dead a few months but...

He glanced around the room. A layer of dust covered the tops of the cluttered furniture. He'd bet nothing had been moved in here in a decade or more.

A picture on top of a large, dark dresser caught his eye. A youngish woman stared hard at the camera, two black braids hanging beside her face. He took a step toward it.

Something about her expression intrigued him. It was impossible to date the picture from her clothes. She wore a blouse and a long skirt like the one Susana had on today.

Aggressive. Her stare was so fierce he could almost

hear her speaking. Curious, he reached out a hand to pick up the tarnished silver frame.

A terrible scream suddenly rang through the apartment, tearing the air and causing Joe to jump back two steps.

"What the hell?"

"Oh, be quiet, Milos." Susana's voice drifted in from the kitchen.

"What?"

A flapping sound made him turn, and for the first time he noticed a large, black birdcage, hung high in one corner of the room.

A big gray parrot glared at him with beady eyes every bit as intense as the woman in the photograph.

It flapped its wings again and a stream of guttural sounds emerged from its mouth in an unsettling mimicry of human speech.

"Milos! I'm warning you." Susana's scolding voice cut through the parrot's squawking.

One beady eye bored into Joe, and he made an effort to stare back just as hard. If you let a parrot stare you down it was pretty much all over.

"Is it saying words?" he asked, once he trusted himself to speak without sounding panicked.

"Yes. But it only speaks Romani."

"What's that?"

"The language of the Rom, the gypsies." Susana emerged into the room bearing two steaming mugs of tea. Her black hair was tossed behind her shoulders, giving him a clear view of her delicate features and habitual serious expression. His body heaved a sigh of relief to see her again. He took a hot mug and nodded his thanks.

"What was he saying?"

"You don't want to know." She gave the parrot a stern look. "But let's just say he's not crazy about you, so far."

"Who's that woman in the picture?" He gestured to the woman with eyes that seemed to claw right into him as he glanced at her again.

"That's my Granna. It was taken not long after she arrived in New York. I think it was supposed to be shown to prospective husbands, though it doesn't seem ideal for that purpose."

"Not unless the idea was to intimidate the heck out of them."

"She was a very strong woman."

"I can see that." Joe blew on his tea. He certainly wasn't going to try picking up that frame again. Or anything else.

Susana sipped her tea. His insides simmered with heat at the sight of her beautiful, unsmiling mouth closing over the ceramic rim.

Uh-oh. He had it bad.

She closed her eyes momentarily as she sipped, and he was assaulted by the image of her writhing under him, eyes closed in blissful ecstasy as he filled her...

He took a quick sip of the punishingly hot liquid.

"Ouch! What is this?" The bitterness puckered his tongue.

"Betel juice tea. My grandmother swore by it." Her thick lashes flickered as she looked up at him.

"For what? Destroying her enemies?"

"You don't like it?" Her mouth quivered with disappointment, triggering a twinge of guilt in Joe.

"Not so far. But maybe it'll grow on me." He sucked his tongue and prepared for another foray into the acrid brew. "What's it supposed to do to you, anyway?"

Susana hesitated, licking her lips in a way that made Joe's hand wobble slightly.

"Ow!" He lifted his scorched hand to suck the hot drops off his skin.

"It has a calming effect."

"You mean like a sleeping draught?" His gut clenched. Was she going to knock him out? *And then what?* He didn't know this woman, didn't know anything about her. For all he knew her grandmother was alive and well in the next room and he was being trapped into some crazy con game...

"No, no, nothing like that." She smiled, her black eyes gleaming with sudden mirth. "It's good for you. And it, er..." She licked her lip thoughtfully, triggering a sudden flow of blood to Joe's groin. "It takes the edge off."

"What edge? You mean stress?"

"Um, yes..." she paused, shooting him a glance that said both "come hither" and "stay back" at the same time. A curl of steam licked up and kissed her face, and Joe suppressed a sudden instinct to do the same.

The rules. Remember the rules.

"The tea calms, it eases, it makes one less...excitable."

"Less...passionate?" He'd begun to sniff out where this was going.

"Yes." A smile flickered across her lips.

"So this tea is insurance against me jumping your bones? You don't trust me to obey your rules."

"It's not that I don't trust you..." She paused, and her eyes flashed a challenge at him.

"You should trust me. I'm a man of my word. If I say I'll do something, then you can damn well believe I'll do it."

But the dark memory of the one time he'd failed to live up to his word suddenly closed over his mind like a hood, threatening to stifle his breath. "If I can do it, I will."

"It's the 'if' part that worries me." Again one slim black brow lifted.

Joe blew out a snort of air. "You think you're pretty irresistible, don't you? Either that or you think I'm so damn desperate I won't be able to keep my hands off you. I'm not some horny kid fresh off a long tour at sea, you know."

"I know." An apologetic tremor hung in her voice, but she tossed her head defiantly, lifting the dark mane of hair for a moment before it settled down her back again.

"I'm thirty years old. I'm divorced. I'm jaded, worn-out, beat-up and not going anywhere fast." He glanced at the steaming mug of pungent tea in his hand, then back up at her. "Believe me, life has taken the edge off me and filed me pretty blunt. I don't need a cup of some witches' brew to do it."

"I'm not a witch." She shot him a look that might have hurt if he didn't have all his shields up right now.

"I didn't say you were. But I'm still not drinking it."

He spotted a mangy looking houseplant sitting on the sill of a lace-hung window, and he strode forward and poured his tea onto the mossy soil. It sank in quickly, steam and bitter fumes rising to insult his nose.

He heard Susana gasp behind him, but when he wheeled around her expression was impassive.

"I guess it'll be interesting to see if that plant is still alive in the morning."

"My grandmother tended that plant for more than twenty years."

"It looks it." Its crinkled brownish leaves looked offended as he turned to glance at it.

"It's a rare herb from the Mongolian steppes. Smoking its leaves promotes mental clarity, strengthens the third eye."

"Do you smoke it?" He couldn't picture Susana rolling a spliff of crinkly brown plant leaves and lighting up. Though the image made a chuckle swell in his belly. He tamped it down.

"No." She stared at him, eyes narrowed, "My third eye is strong enough already."

A chill seized him, as if he suddenly expected a third eye to appear in the middle of her smooth forehead.

"You won't miss the plant then," he quipped, lifting his chin.

"No. I suppose I won't." Susana very deliberately took another sip of her tea. "I'm not good at letting go of stuff, either."

"It's not easy to get rid of things when a person has died. I know my mom kept my dad's closet just as he'd left it. She couldn't bring herself to throw anything away."

"How long before she changed it?"

Joe sucked in a breath. "I don't suppose she ever did. She died a couple of years after he did. I was away at sea, though. Everything was gone when I got back."

The dull ache of that pain still tugged at him. He'd kissed his mom goodbye, left his childhood home...and never seen either of them again.

"Oh." Concern wrinkled Susana's brow. "That's terrible. What happened?"

"The landlord needed to rent the place, I guess. He kept some photos for me, important papers, that kind of thing. It's okay with me. I don't need a lot of stuff to remember them by."

"People you love are always with you, aren't they?" Her eyes searched his face, hungry for solace.

"Yes," he said, trying to reassure her, wishing he could reassure himself.

All in all, he'd rather think about her breasts.

"So where am I sleeping?"

"Um," she licked her lips nervously. He liked thinking about those, too. His jeans tightened again. "I guess I'll put you in Granna's room."

His jeans suddenly grew loose. "Oh-kay. Think Granna would mind?"

"Undoubtedly." She giggled nervously. "But she's not here to complain."

Joe wasn't so sure. The stern warning her picture had glared at him made her presence uncomfortably vivid. And then there was her parrot.

He glanced at the feathered monster perched on its bar in the menacing cage. It shifted from foot to foot, eyeing him, but mercifully keeping its thoughts to itself.

"Are you afraid?" A smile quirked the corner of Susana's mouth.

"Never." He drew in a breath and rose to his full height. Jeez, it was a New York City tenement building. People were going about their business in their own apartments not more than three yards away.

Funny how he couldn't hear any sounds from outside the apartment. Not even traffic.

Must be double glazing.

"Would you like to see the room?"

"Sure." His stomach tightened, but he forced a smile.

"This way. She turned, her skirt twirling behind her and momentarily molding itself to the curve of her backside.

Ah, that's more like it.

A flush of warmth soothed him as he followed her through the apartment.

Susana drew in a quick breath as she placed her hand on the doorknob. She turned it and flung the door open wide as if trying to banish demons.

Joe bit the inside of his mouth hard and leaned forward to peer in.

"Oh."

The single word escaped him as he absorbed the shock of seeing a totally white space, devoid of furniture except for a single bed spread with a plain white spread.

He wasn't sure what he'd expected but that wasn't it.

"Where's all the stuff?"

Still hovering in the doorway, Susana looked at him, a little apprehensive. "It is a gypsy tradition to burn all a person's belongings after they die."

"So you burned all the stuff in her bedroom."

She nodded. "I know it must seem odd…"

"What seems odd is that you only burned the stuff in here but left the rest of the apartment piled high with clutter. It sounds like you had a great opportunity to redecorate from the ground up."

"You're coldhearted, Joe." Her accusatory stare made his heart bump.

"I know."

Coldhearted and hot blooded, he thought, as he watched her chest heave beneath her T-shirt. She was struggling to contain some emotion she didn't want to share, and all he could think about was the inviting roundness of her curves.

Maybe he should have drunk the tea after all. He *should* be ashamed of himself. Then again, it was reassuring that at least one part of him was still in good working order. Unlike his heart and his head.

He couldn't remember the last time he'd even noticed a woman. He'd thought all those kinds of instincts had dried out and shriveled up along with his faith in humanity. But Susana had got his blood pumping again.

Maybe there was hope for him after all.

"If you don't want to sleep in here, I understand." Her wary expression belied her calm voice.

"I'd be happy to sleep here. Looks good to me," he lied.

Susana forced a tight smile. "Great. Let me get you a candle. The overhead light doesn't work."

Joe stepped into the room and dumped his leather bag on the floor beside the bed. He raised his arms over his head and stretched, joints cracking loud as he flexed his muscles. What the heck, he'd had enough of hotel rooms.

And this room came with the promise of breakfast with Susana.

She returned with a thick white candle in a tarnished brass holder. She lit it with a match and placed it on the floor next to the bed.

"I hope you don't need to get a lot of reading done." She shrugged apologetically. "Granna didn't like electric light."

"Sleep is top on my agenda."

"Is there any particular time you'd like me to wake you?"

"Any time you want." He winked. And regretted it when she stiffened and looked at him sternly.

"I'll be locking my bedroom door."

Joe chuckled. "You really don't trust me, do you?"

"Not much. I like you though." Her hair hid her

sudden smile as she twirled away from him and exited the room, closing the door behind her.

Joe sank down onto the bed, a goofy smile spreading across his face. He liked her, too. She'd taken a chance on him, which is something no one else had been willing to do lately.

He eased off his shoes and jeans and stretched out on his back, hands behind his head, elbows akimbo. Trying to relax.

The candle flame guttered a bit in an invisible breeze, casting long shadows over the plain white walls. Spooky. This whole apartment was kind of spooky. Susana was pretty spooky, too, truth be told.

Adrenaline snaked through him as he sniffed the air.

Did he imagine it, or was there a cloyingly sweet aroma of incense curling its way under the door?

She must have lit something out there. Hopefully it wouldn't make his balls shrivel up like raisins while he slept. Wouldn't have worried him yesterday but now there was a chance he might need them again.

Or not. Susana didn't seem like the type to put out easily. Or at all.

Was she a virgin? Probably.

But how long would she stay one?

The question tickled his imagination and warmed his tired body as he sank into an exhausted slumber.

Susana sat awkwardly on her bed, fists buried in the folds of her nightgown, listening for any hint of sound that might sneak through the wall from Granna's room.

From Joe's room.

Her body tingled with excitement at the thought of Joe's big body stretched out on the bed.

Of his guttural breathing, snoring maybe, stirring the

air with its masculine vibrations.

But the thick plaster walls of the old building meant she could hear them only in her imagination. An imagination that had suddenly become shockingly vivid.

Granna had warned her against exercising it. The veil between fantasy and reality could be very thin, she cautioned. One moment you're thinking something, the next you're doing it.

Which was all very well if you were just looking to marry and settle down and raise children. But quite another if you had an important gift to nurture. Susana knew a gift like hers came along only once every three generations. Even though she was only half Rom, she was the one who'd inherited the powers.

It had changed her life when she'd found out. Before that she'd been the half-breed, the mistake, lovingly tolerated by her grandmother as an accident of cruel fate.

But once they both realized she had the third eye, she'd instantly been granted new status in the gypsy world.

It had happened around the time of puberty, the time of sexual stirrings and emotional awakenings. As her body blossomed into a woman's, so her mind developed its strange and potent ability to see beyond the present. So her long-standing engagement had been cancelled and all of her grandmother's energies channeled into helping her develop a gift that was—so they said—peerless in her generation.

The gift that had presented her with the vision of herself and Joe, walking hand in hand.

She lay slowly back on the bed. The warm air coaxed her to remove her nightgown and she slipped it off.

Her skin glowed in the moonlight sneaking through

the thin curtains. Her body hummed with unfamiliar arousal, and fear. She'd often slept naked, but never with a man in the next room. Certainly not a man whose destiny intertwined dangerously with hers.

Dangerous because to act on her desires could mean forsaking her gift.

It didn't always happen, but it was usually observed in her family that once a girl became a woman—once she joined with a man—she lost her ability to see into the future and became a prisoner of the here and now.

A willing prisoner, usually. Most women preferred the companionship of a husband and children to the lonely solitude of a visionary. They used their gifts while they had them, then they readily gave them up and took on the happier role of wife and mother.

Once a woman was past the hustle and bustle of the child-rearing years, especially if she was widowed, the gift sometimes returned. This had been the case with her grandmother.

The grandmother who had told her to cling to her gifts at all costs. They were too powerful, too precious to sacrifice for the transient comforts of a family. *Don't get involved with a man. You'll regret it*, she'd said.

And Susana had always believed her.

Until now.

The scent of him warned her of his presence before she could make out his silhouette in the darkened room. A stirring, musky aroma—hot unvarnished maleness—against the backdrop of the incense she'd lit to smooth out the atmosphere.

Her eyes snapped open, searching the darkness for its source. Just then the mattress shifted, tipping her, as his weight settled heavily onto it.

Fear triggered her upright, naked, every nerve in her body on full alert.

The man on her bed didn't stir. She saw the gleam of his eyes in the thin reflected moonlight. Dark eyes in the dark night.

Her fingers sang with the urge to leap to her breasts and cover them. But strangely her arms continued to hang by her sides.

The broad, masculine silhouette in front of her shifted slightly, then lifted a powerful arm. Her nipples tightened as his hand traversed the darkness between them, fingers rising toward her exposed breasts.

She'd never been more vulnerable.

Or more intrigued.

She gasped as his fingertips made contact with the tiny hairs on her skin, his touch so soft she could barely feel it. Then the pressure grew deeper, the pads of his fingers sinking into the soft flesh, his palm sliding gently under her breast to cup its weight.

His thumb settled against her nipple, chafing slightly until she blinked in the darkness, her breath coming faster as the odd sensation heated her blood.

I like you.

She'd thrown the words behind her as she turned away from him. Apparently they'd fallen like bread crumbs on a woodland trail, beckoning him to follow.

She wasn't sure why she'd said them at the time. Except that they were the truth.

She wasn't even sure why she liked him. Just that she did.

He raised his other hand toward her untouched breast. She drew in a quick breath as her nipple stung with anticipation of his touch.

She leaned forward a little, her body unconsciously

encouraging his caress. His gaze was no more than a gleam in the darkness, his expression invisible. But she heard his breathing hitch as his fingertips grazed the side of her breast, sliding down to her waist.

What do you want from me?

Sensitive nerve endings shimmered under his gentle touch. Her insides heated and softened, her resistance lowering every second.

Her arms stirred at her sides, wanting to reach out, wanting to claim him, too. She lifted a tentative hand and watched her fingers, pale in the moonlight, as she raised it to touch his mouth.

As her fingertips met his lips they parted, and his hot breath tickled her skin. Her chin lifted as a sudden wave of desire rose through her at the thought of that scorching breath trailing, very slowly, all over her body.

What do you want from him, Susana?

Do you want to give up your powers? Do you want to give yourself to this man—just for one night—and wake up an ordinary girl?

Her gifts were not merely an entertaining talent; they were her livelihood. She didn't know how to do anything else. Her hand slid back to her side.

But the mattress tilted her toward Joe as he eased his weight along it, closing the distance between them.

Susana knelt on top of the sheets, in the same position she'd sprung to when she realized he was there. As he shifted closer, his knee bumped softly against her thigh.

She could see the gleam of his smile in the darkness. She smiled back.

He'd broken into her locked room. Who did that but a thief? He'd come to steal something from her, something he didn't even know he had the power to take.

But he knew she was a virgin. She could see that.

Her lack of sexual experience had always been a badge of pride she'd worn, a symbol of her apartness. *You are special,* her grandmother had said. *Not like those other girls.* She'd held her head high as they'd snickered behind their hands.

One by one the girls she'd grown up with had gotten married. By the time she was twenty-one she was the only girl in the extended family who had no man of her own.

Now she was the only one who lived alone.

Which was not a natural state of affairs for a gypsy.

Joe's callused palms grazed her skin as they slid down the sides of her torso to ring her slender waist. She held her breath as his fingertips drifted over the soft flesh of her belly, causing a tremor inside her empty womb.

Don't you ever want to have a baby? her girl cousins had asked, eyes wide with astonishment.

No.

And she'd always meant it when her grandmother was alive, assuring her of the paramount importance of developing her third eye, the life of the mind supplanting the life of the body.

Joe's hand slid lower, fingertips diving into the dark shadow of hair between her legs. Susana gasped. Little quakes of sensation shivered at the base of her thighs, sticky heat gathering between her legs.

Don't you want to make love with a man? they'd asked.

No, she'd always said.

Joe leaned forward, and her eyes slid shut as his mouth closed over hers in a hot, hungry kiss that stole her breath.

Yes.

Her nerves crackled with the strange and frightening response.

She wanted to give herself to Joe. A man who came with no promises, no assurances, no marriage contract. A man who demanded no dowry, no proud unbroken lineage, no lifetime of faithful bondage.

Joe pulled back, leaving her breathless, and her eyes sprang open. Heat shimmered between them as his face hovered only inches from hers in the darkness.

Instinctively, her arms rose from her sides and snaked around his neck, pulling him to her. Her fingers probed into his thick dark hair, relishing the coarse texture of it. She lifted her face to his unshaved cheek, enjoying its rough surface, teasing and pricking her lips over the unfamiliar masculine edge of his cheekbone.

Her breath came in shallow gasps, her body so stoked with desire she thought it might burst into flame at any second.

Joe's big hands cupped her buttocks, raising her up, unsettling her and threatening to topple her onto him.

As he lifted her, one hand slid between her legs, into the moist warmth. Her mouth fell open and a soft moan hung in the air between them as a thick finger penetrated the wetness, filling her.

Shuddering, she felt herself already losing control. Muscles seized, already pulsing in an urgent rhythm as she fell onto him, clinging, her breath lost against his rough, musky skin.

And even as her body quivered with fierce aftershocks the questions rang in her mind.

Does it count? Am I no longer a virgin?

Eyes squeezed shut she held Joe tight as she focused

all her energies on seeing with her third eye.

Nothing.

Terror seized her. Icy fingers gripped at her heart as she realized she'd just given up everything. Given up her life, her past, her future, everything, for a few brief moments of pleasure with a man she barely knew.

And then she woke up. Alone.

4

Joe stretched and squinted his eyes against the sun streaming in through the uncovered windows. The curtains must have been burned along with the rest of the stuff.

Whatever was in that incense had knocked him out cold. Or maybe he was just so dog tired he'd really needed a good night's rest. Whichever, it was the first decent night of sleep he'd had in a long time. No nightmares either, which was a freakin' miracle.

He rolled out of bed and wandered into the hallway in search of the bathroom.

"Ahh!" The shriek made him jump.

"Morning, Susana."

She gave him a quick look of horror and scuttled away.

"Morning," she whispered harshly from the living room.

He glanced down at his underwear. He was fully covered, nothing untoward going on. He shrugged and pushed into the bathroom.

Ouch. A glimpse in the mirror was not a pretty sight. Time to break out the razor. But it wasn't like he'd suddenly grown horns—what had gotten her all rattled?

He showered, shaved, dressed in clean clothes and was feeling almost completely human by the time he ventured into the kitchen in search of Susana.

He'd heard pans clattering and the rousing aroma of bacon filled the air. A smile started to creep across his face in anticipation of seeing her, and he wiped it away. Didn't want to look like a wolf entering a sheep pen this early in the morning.

"Something smells good."

"Just bacon and eggs. Would you like toast with it?"

"Love some. Can I help?"

She shook her head in response and indicated for him to sit at the tiny table pushed into the corner of the small kitchen. He eased himself down into the tight space and propped his elbows on the table.

He seized the opportunity to get a good look at Susana. Again she wore a long, full skirt, dark, with a pattern of tiny flowers. On top, a black blouse tucked in to reveal her slender waist. Her thick, shiny hair hid her face from him as she bent over the task of scrambling the eggs.

Did she know concealment did far more to inflame his imagination than if she'd put everything on display? A tantalizing flash of slim ankle and her narrow bare feet were all he could see of what could only be long, shapely legs.

She had a nice curve to her hip, too. Hourglass.

Down boy.

He shifted in his chair as his blood heated before the sun had even had a chance to steam up the apartment.

"Would you like tea? I'm afraid I don't have coffee."

"No thanks." He wasn't taking any more chances with her teas. "Milk would be great if you have it. Otherwise water's fine."

Her skirt flew out behind her as she darted to the fridge and retrieved the milk. She seemed all on edge this morning, her movements quick and jerky. He still hadn't gotten a good look at her face yet.

But there was no way she could keep it hidden as she turned to him with a full glass of milk. She carried it carefully, eyes focused on the white liquid as she set the glass down on the table.

Their eyes met for an instant as she looked up, black gaze wide and startled. She blinked and wheeled away, silent feet hurrying back to the stove.

Joe shrugged and stretched. Women. No telling what she was all wound up about. Probably had nothing to do with him anyway.

"Thanks for letting me sleep over. Best night of sleep I've had in a long time."

"You're welcome." Her voice emerged as a throaty whisper, and she cleared her throat as she turned to him with a steaming plate of eggs, bacon and toast.

"Damn, that looks good!"

A quick smile flashed across her face at his compliment. She set the plate down on the table, then hesitated for a second with her hands on her hips.

"Aren't you going to join me?"

"I had something to eat earlier." She raised a hand to push back her hair, her movements still hesitant, edgy.

"Will you sit with me?"

Something had changed since last night. Since that odd but lovely moment when she'd told him she liked him. He didn't want her off scuttling around the apartment, not looking him in the eye, then shoving him out the door without really facing him.

She bit her lip, hands still on her hips. "Okay." She yanked out the chair, then sat down quickly, adjusting her full skirt about her legs.

He scooped up a big forkful of eggs and shoved it into his mouth. She watched him suspiciously as he chewed.

"S'good."

"I'm glad." She licked her lips and shifted a little.

"Would you like a bite?" He proffered a forkful of bacon and eggs.

A shy smile curved her lips. "No, thanks. You eat it."

"Okay." He forked the breakfast into his smiling mouth and chewed it, watching her. She blinked nervously.

"Your grandma didn't haunt me last night."

"Did you think she would?"

"It seemed like a possibility."

She smiled. "I was a little worried, too, since we didn't burn her bed. It's metal. She never much liked sleeping in bed, though."

"Where did she sleep?"

"On the couch in the living room mostly. She usually fell asleep during *Law & Order*."

Their chuckles mingled, and the tension lifted slightly.

"Did you burn the sofa?"

She nodded. "In the fireplace. My cousin Roman chopped it up with an axe."

"I bet the neighbors enjoyed that."

"The neighbors don't bother us."

"Yeah, 'cos they think you'll put a curse on them."

"Probably."

"Have you ever put a curse on anyone?" A little twinge of anticipation tightened his belly.

She paused, looked at him slyly, a smile playing across her lips. "Maybe."

"You wouldn't put one on me, would you?" He hoped his tone sounded light.

She didn't answer right away. She studied his face and her eyes narrowed slightly. "You may not like this..." She paused and licked her lips thoughtfully. "But I think you're under a curse already."

"Yeah, well, you may have a point there." He tried to sound jovial as he shoved more food in his mouth.

"I'm serious."

"I bet you're always pretty serious."

Her shoulders hitched in a tiny shrug. "You don't have to listen to me. You didn't pay me for my advice, and you don't have to take it."

"Just to keep it lively, what would be your advice?"

"First, you need to find the root of the curse, where it's taken hold."

"Wait a second here." Joe held up a hand as he finished chewing and swallowed his mouthful. "Are you trying to say someone out there has actually put a curse on me?"

"Not necessarily." She regarded him steadily, her heart-shaped face solemn. Calm repose had replaced her flightiness of earlier. She was on her own turf now.

Joe's gut tightened again. "Well?"

"A curse can come into being without deliberate ill will on the part of any one person."

"You mean it can just spring to life?"

"Not exactly, it's hard to explain." She rearranged the bracelets on her wrist, hesitating. Then she looked back up at him cautiously. "If you lose faith in yourself, that can function as a curse."

"Like a self-fulfilling prophecy?"

She nodded. "Kind of."

He'd lost faith in himself all right. Not all at once. It

had been nibbled away in tiny bites until there just wasn't any more left. But he didn't want to tell his pretty gypsy girl about all that stuff. Didn't want to think about it either.

Damn she was pretty. He loved her serious expression, no simpering and flirting for her. Getting into her pants might cure what ailed him. Not that she wore pants. Getting under that big skirt then. Maybe she'd let him crawl right under it and hide down there. Make a long slow acquaintance with her thighs.

"If the root of the curse can be found, it can be removed." Her eyes narrowed.

Joe's attention drifted reluctantly back to their conversation. "How do you get to the bottom of it?"

"By doing a reading."

"No thanks. Been there, done that."

She reached a hand across the table. On impulse he dropped his fork and took it. She curled her fingers around his palm and pressed her cool fingertips lightly into his warm flesh.

"It's okay, Joe."

"I look that bad, huh?"

"I can see from your face that you have been badly hurt."

"Yeah, well, that's life."

"The curse can be lifted."

"I still don't believe there is a curse."

"I know, and that's okay, too." She squeezed his hand gently, dark eyes filled with compassion.

Joe clamped his teeth down on the inside of his mouth, trying to bite back the surge of emotion welling inside him. He hadn't yet embarrassed himself by bawling in front of anyone, and he didn't plan to start now.

He lifted his chin, trying to get his head up above dangerous waters. "You think you can see right through me, don't you?"

"No. I can only see the surface, just like anyone else. But from my work I have much experience with people...who need help."

"You think I need help?" He accompanied his words with a dismissive snort.

"Yes. You wouldn't have come back to me if you didn't."

"I don't even know why I came to you. But I can think of one thing you could help me with."

"What's that?"

She said it so sincerely, with such an expression of thoughtful concern, that he couldn't bring himself to say the crude, sexually suggestive words he'd hoped to brush her off with.

"You could let go of my hand so I can finish my breakfast."

She gave him a knowing smile as she withdrew her hand gently from his.

He picked up his fork and stuffed another heaping mouthful of bacon and eggs into his mouth. Narrow escape. He'd come way too close to losing it right there. He was walking a fine line between sanity and madness lately, and he wasn't sure this chick was going to help him fall on the right side of the line if he crashed.

He glanced up at her and got an odd little stab in his gut when he saw she was looking at him, soft-eyed, her lips curved in a slight smile.

"What're you smiling about?"

"Nothing."

"I guess we can both play at that game, huh?"

She nodded, still smiling like the Mona Lisa, and he

got on with eating his breakfast.

Susana got up and wandered off while Joe finished up the last of his eggs. He stretched as best he could in the cramped space. Damn he felt relaxed. And good. Whatever tricks she had up her sleeve, so far they were working.

But he had work to do today. He needed to find a place to live and start getting his business plan off the ground. And he had to deposit that check.

The thought of the check, still crumpled in the back pocket of yesterday's jeans, stirred his muscles to life. He really shouldn't leave that kind of money lying around.

He squeezed himself out from behind the table and carried his plate and glass to the sink. Common politeness told him to wash up, but suddenly he had a very strong desire to make sure his check was where he left it.

Not that he didn't trust Susana or anything.

Anxiety pricked him as he strode into the hallway and shoved open the door to Grandma's bedroom. Phew. Everything looked much as he'd left it. He snuck a glance at the doorway before picking his crumpled jeans off the floor and shoving his hand into the back pocket.

Empty.

Jesus.

He groped for the other pocket, heart firing. When his fingers closed around the crisp paper he let out an audible sigh of relief.

"Thought I robbed you?"

Susana's cool voice from the doorway made him jump.

"No."

"You think all gypsies are thieves?"

"No, I don't."

"Yes, you do. I saw you come running in here to check your pockets after I got up."

"If you put it that way, I have pretty solid evidence that all humans are thieves and will strip you bare sooner or later."

He stared at her for a second, and she regarded him down the length of her elegant nose. Heating with embarrassment, Joe balled up his jeans and flung them at his bag, then tucked the check into the front pocket of his clean jeans.

"Hmm. Perhaps you're right. Perhaps it's best not to trust anyone."

She stood regally in the doorway, chin lifted. Joe could hear doors slamming shut in her mind. He'd obviously just dropped a thousand notches in her esteem.

There went his chances of getting under her skirt.

"I appreciate you letting me sleep over." His own chin tilted naturally as he turned to her, defying her to look down on him.

Not that she could, since he was several inches taller. But her quiet dignity gave her stature beyond her physical height.

"It was nothing." The emphasis on the last word cut him like a blunt knife.

"How can I repay you?"

She laughed. The sound of it curdled his breakfast. "Don't worry. I'll just help myself."

Joe felt his heart literally sinking. He didn't realize until this moment, but overnight he'd come to count on Susana's friendship. And now she'd withdrawn it.

The renewed sense of aloneness chilled him. His

calm relaxation of a few minutes ago evaporated as the familiar tension crept back into his muscles, tightening them. Girding him for battle with a cruel world.

"Look, I didn't mean to insult you, Susana. It's just that this piece of paper," he fished into his pocket and drew it out. "It's all the money I have in the world."

She raised an eyebrow very slightly over her withering glance.

He unfolded the crumpled and insignificant looking blue paper.

"It's a check."

"I can see that." She crossed her arms over her chest.

"For one million, nine hundred and seventy two thousand dollars."

Her eyes widened. "That's a lot of dough."

"You're telling me. You can see why I'm a little antsy about it."

"You should be. Why are you carrying that kind of money around in your pocket?"

"I was on my way to the bank when I stumbled across this gypsy fortune-teller."

"Banks aren't open in the evening."

"No? Guess it's okay I didn't make it there, then."

Susana planted her hands on her hips and stared at him. The expression on her face softened. She glanced down at the blue paper then back up at him. "What's it from?"

"I sold my business. Well, my share of it anyway."

To the thieving swine who stole my wife.

A spark of rage stirred his gut, and he blew out a breath. No sense getting all riled up any more. It was over. Cold hard cash, that was all he had left to worry about now.

"Huh." She pursed her lips. "Must be nice to have

that kind of money."

Joe shrugged. "I wouldn't know. I haven't cashed it yet."

"What kind of business was it?"

"Security."

She raised an eyebrow but didn't ask for details. "What are you going to do with it?"

Joe suppressed a chuckle. She was pretty interested all of a sudden. "I dunno. Maybe we could go to Atlantic City and see if I can double it?"

Her eyes narrowed, and he saw her fighting to keep a smile from creeping across her lips.

"I'm serious. I'm a desperate man, remember?"

"Not that desperate. You'd better get that to the bank before someone less trustworthy than me relieves you of it."

"Yeah. I guess I'd better. You want to come?"

He watched her hesitate, her eyes suddenly bright. Jeez, maybe she did like the idea of sticking close to all that money? He didn't much mind, though. As long as she was back on his side.

"Come on, I need you, Susana, I don't even know which bank to go to. You can pick one for me. But then I don't suppose gypsies go in for banks much. Do you keep all your money under the bed?"

"I wear it around my neck in gold coins, of course." A smile tugged at her lips again.

"All right. Maybe we can get this melted down into some coins and you can wear them for me?"

"Sounds kind of heavy."

"Weight-bearing exercise is good for the bones."

"You're terrible, Joe."

"I know. That's why I'm so damn miserable."

She tossed her head, the mane of raven hair falling

down her back. "I'll come to the bank with you."

"Now you know I'm loaded you want to be my friend again?"

"Something like that."

"I'll take what I can get."

Joe watched as she locked up the apartment. Five locks seemed a little paranoid, but he enjoyed watching her bend over to turn the one right near the floor.

Sooner or later, he was going to get under that skirt. Preferably sooner.

"You can leave your bag here, you know."

"Nah, it's got stuff in it I might need."

"You don't trust me?" Her brow arched but her expression was warm.

"Let's not go down that road again. And who knows, I might not be back. I'm going to look for an apartment today." He looked at her quickly to gauge her reaction.

And was delighted to see a flicker of alarm—and very definite disappointment—cross her delicate features.

"Maybe you could help me find it?"

"I have to get to the store. I have an appointment at ten-thirty. But if you do need a place to stay tonight..." She pulled the key out of the last lock and pushed past him to the stairs. Her hair flew out behind her as she dashed down the first flight.

"If I need a place to stay tonight?"

She turned around and put her finger to her lips, giving him a stern glare. Joe glanced around at the closed apartment doors ringing the narrow stairwell. He nodded and smiled.

"Cool."

She dashed down the stairs so fast he had to jump them two at a time to keep up with her. No wonder she kept so trim.

"Hey, wait up!" he shouted, as she pushed out the door into the blinding brightness of the street.

She strode along the sidewalk, skirt flying behind her. An invitation to hot pursuit. Exhilaration jumped in Joe's veins as he smelled the sea in the warm morning air—salt and seaweed and life.

He dashed past Susana, then turned and blocked her. She bumped into him, hair flying, breasts crushing deliciously against his hard chest.

"Ouch!" Her eyes glittered.

Joe dropped his bag and wrapped his arms round her, imprisoning her with his body.

"We're not in your apartment any more. The rules are lifted."

Her fingers tightened around his biceps, holding him at bay. "We're out in the street."

"I know."

"People are watching." Her eyes darted about his face.

"Do you care?"

She hesitated, teeth grazing her lip. "Not really."

"Me neither." He held her gaze for a minute as her pupils darkened with desire. "I'd like to kiss you."

She tossed her hair, releasing a whiff of incense from its black depths.

Her fingers softened their grip but her wrists held firm. Pushing him back until her breasts were one or two inches from his chest.

From his heart. Which tightened, beating harder as heat crept through his muscles.

He'd kept himself firmly in the "off" position all night. Playing by the rules.

Her lips pressed together, skeptical. But her eyes

were an invitation that summoned him to act.

Joe buried his face in the crook of her neck, inhaling the exotic scent as her hair trailed over her face. He heard her swift intake of breath as he brushed her earlobe with his lips.

"I'd like to make love to you." He whispered it so softly the words were barely more than breath.

She gasped and stiffened.

"Not now," he whispered, lips brushing the pulse below her ear. "Now I just want to kiss you."

He trailed his lips over her cheekbone, her skin smooth, silky and cool under his mouth. His arms held her tightly to prevent escape. He couldn't bear to lose her now.

All night he'd held thoughts of her at bay. Visions of her that danced at the edges of his mind, taunting and teasing him. Curious thoughts about every hidden inch of her.

He'd played by the rules.

He hadn't thought about the tiny dimple in the middle of her chin that deepened when she smiled. Or about her long, elegant fingers tipped with gloriously unvarnished shell-pink nails.

Or about the thighs that strode under her long skirt.

As his lips neared the corner of her mouth, her eyes flickered closed, black lashes falling like a curtain. Her lips softened, flushed with new blood.

While they were on her turf, he'd been good.

He hadn't entertained the tiniest notion of finding her belly button in the dark, with his tongue. He hadn't dreamed about exploring every inch of her with the sensitive tip of his nose, seeking the subtle private scents, the sweet, musky animal smells that must lie under that seductive veil of incense. He hadn't fantasized about her lips.

But now he parted them with a soft lick of his tongue.

A tiny moan escaped. Her nails dug into his skin—a sweet agony that melded with the blissful sensation of losing his mouth in hers.

Then her fingers crept up his arms, and suddenly those mysterious breasts were pressing against his chest as her fingers threaded into hair.

Joe released a groan that got lost in the hot darkness of their kiss.

He'd kept himself in the "off" position all night long, but as his tongue roamed into Susana's hot, welcoming mouth, "on" roared through his blood in a torrent that threatened to knock him off his feet.

His palms slid down into the hollow above her buttocks. He could feel the teasing lift of muscle where the sweet curve of her backside began and he fought to keep his hands from sliding down to cup their soft roundness.

You're in public.

His body didn't care. Buried in the folds of Susana's skirt, his jeans bulged. Tightness hummed in his nerves as his body came alive with dangerous arousal.

He shuddered as she licked his tongue. She'd softened, losing herself in the kiss, her hands drifting through his hair and down over his face. Her breasts crushed against him, braless and unrestrained, her nipples grazing his own as she strained upward on tiptoe.

One long finger trailed over his cheek and plunged into his mouth, breaking the vacuum of their kiss and probing along with her tongue in an act of unashamed discovery that almost made him lose it right there on a city sidewalk.

He clung to her to keep upright now, his arousal so intense that reality shimmered beyond his grasp. She withdrew her wet finger and dragged it down over his T-shirt, suddenly pinching his nipple hard as she reached it.

Joe jerked back, a wordless shout forming on his lips as they lost contact with hers.

His eyes shot open and he saw her face, just inches from his, her eyes black with desire. She panted, her breath coming in tiny gasps, her mouth open. She blinked rapidly and suddenly her hands flew to cover her swollen red lips.

The moment was over.

Joe dragged a hand through his hair, trying to catch his own breath. Trying to catch thoughts that flew wildly around him. His body stung with the unwelcoming parting from the soft, female flesh it ached so badly for.

"I'm sorry!" Susana's eyes were wide with horror now.

"Don't be sorry."

"I hurt you. I don't know what..." She shook her head, struggling for words. "I've never..." She dropped her head, still shaking it, her hair tossing about her face as she struggled for breath and words.

"It was magic," he said, and reached his hand out to cup her chin and lift it. "I've never..." He shook his head too, still trying to untangle his messed-up thoughts. "I've never...either. Never like that. That was something else."

He had no idea what he was trying to say. The physical sensations torturing his body were totally new. He was no virgin for sure, but he'd never known the torment of such severe and intense arousal.

Of such unexpected and intriguing behavior by a woman.

But Susana was no ordinary woman. He knew that before he kissed her.

And now he suspected he'd run aground on the tip of an iceberg that would change his life forever.

Susana stepped back from him. "I'm embarrassed."

"Don't be." He blew out a breath of air as his glance jerked down to his bulging jeans. He quickly untucked his T-shirt to cover his very obvious arousal.

Susana pushed her hair off her face. Two pink spots high on her cheeks shone through her honey complexion. She bit a swollen red lip.

"I have to go... My appointment."

"I know. Can I see you again? Can I come by later?"

His chest constricted. He couldn't hear a no. If she said it, he'd come anyway.

Susana glanced about, suddenly aware of the street around them. Of the people pointedly ignoring them.

"Yes." She breathed it, surreptitious, a secret message.

Joe let out an audible exhale of relief. "I'll come here around seven, okay?"

"Yes." She still looked dazed, as if she'd just staggered out of a burning building. "The buzzer's broken. Just call up. I'll leave the window open."

A grin swept across his face. "You'll hear me."

He didn't know what to say next. Certainly not "goodbye." "See you later" was far too casual.

"You're beautiful."

Susana's eyes widened for a second before she gasped and took off down the block, running.

Joe stared as her skirt flared out behind her and her

hair tossed about her shoulder blades until she rounded the corner and vanished from sight.

5

He'd gone to the bank alone. Deposited his check despite gaping disbelief and admonitions that no withdrawal could be made until it cleared. Whatever.

With a cash advance on his credit card he'd rented a nice apartment right on the water in Tribeca.

Was he excited about having a truckload of money and a snazzy waterfront loft? Nope.

Was he excited about seeing Susana again?

Hell, yeah.

He strode along Canal Street, whistling. Sailors were supposed to whistle, weren't they? He wasn't a sailor any more, and they'd been as glad to get rid of him as he was to get out. But that was all in the past. Suddenly he was setting sail on a new adventure and he'd whistle if he wanted to, dammit.

Canal Street thronged with people. Conversation buzzed and squawked around him in fifty languages. Huge dead fish on ice stared up at him, and rap thundered out of customized woofers as he wove through the crowds.

He picked up Chinese takeout as he strolled though Chinatown, still whistling. Tomorrow he'd call his contacts and line up some potential clients. His reputation should be enough to get him started, even in the competitive field of corporate Internet security. And because it was a different market it wouldn't affect the no-compete clause he'd signed with his former business partner.

His former best friend. He threw back his shoulders and inhaled a deep breath of steamy city air. *Don't look back.* One foot in front of the other. Keep on movin'.

Thoughts of Susana were a nice distraction. Thoughts of her almond-shaped black eyes. Of her long, prying fingers. Of her slim ankles and the world of mystery hidden by her long skirt.

Would the rules still be in place? Probably. But that was okay. He could wait.

At least he thought he could. He couldn't tell quite what was going to happen with Susana around.

He laughed aloud, careless of what anyone thought. He was one more crazy man on an island full of crazy people, and that was okay too. He hadn't felt this good in a long, long time.

Hope. That's what Susana had given back to him. A little taste of it went a long way right now.

He crossed Delancy Street and strode along Susana's block, heart thumping with anticipation. Merengue music pumping out the open windows of a car tickled his feet into a rhythm.

He stopped in front of Susana's building. An ordinary brick walk-up, like all the others on the street. He couldn't even see her top-floor window from where he stood in front of the doorway, so he crossed the street for a better view. Yellowed lace covered all the windows, but one was propped open. The lace flapped a little in the evening breeze.

She was waiting for him.

He put the plastic bag of Chinese takeout carefully down on the sidewalk next to him and cupped his hands around his mouth.

"Rapunzel! Rapunzel!"

He grinned, watching the curtains. Wondered how carefully she was listening. When they flicked aside right away, he laughed aloud. Susana's face appeared beneath the lace, smiling.

"The buzzer doesn't work. I'll come down."

He picked up the Chinese and crossed the street. Almost as soon as he got there the front door swung open and Susana met him with a smile as broad as his own.

"Hi."

"Hi." Oh, lord, he felt like a teenager on his first date. Acting like one, too. "I brought dinner." He lifted the bag.

"Thanks." Her lips pressed together as she struggled to suppress her smile. "So I'm Rapunzel, am I?"

"You live in a brick tower, and you've got long hair."

"Not long enough, though, or I'd have saved you climbing the stairs." She fought back another smile and turned to the stairs, then leaped them two at a time. Joe was glad of the opportunity to run up, since his whole body pounded with unspent adrenaline.

Incense hung in the air of the apartment, swirling amid the dust stirred up by their breathless entry. As soon as Joe entered he saw the parrot, shifting uneasily from foot to foot in its big black cage as it fixed one gleaming eye on him.

"Hello, Polly," he said lightly.

The parrot let forth a stream of obvious invective in whatever guttural language it spoke.

"Milos!" Susana lifted a finger of warning at the

parrot's cage. Milos lifted his feathered wings in a threatening gesture and shook his head vigorously, all without taking his eye off Joe.

"Guess he's not too happy to see me again."

"He's never happy about anything."

Joe glanced at the bureau where the picture of Grandma stood. She didn't look happy to see him either. "I brought General Tsao's chicken," he announced to the photograph.

Susana chuckled. "Come into the kitchen. We'll eat."

He told her about his business plan while they ate dinner. She looked impressed. Intrigued. She asked him how he'd managed to make so much money when he'd been out of the Navy only three years. He told her that the work he'd done in the service—systems security—had given him a unique skill set in high demand by corporations.

"So you are a rich man, and you plan to become richer." Her eyes shone.

"Yeah. You like that?"

She shrugged. "What I think makes no difference."

"Unless you think our destinies are still linked in some way." He raised his eyebrows suggestively. Maybe the mysterious hand of fate would get him under her skirt.

She held his gaze. "There's only one way to find out."

"What's that?"

She narrowed her eyes slightly, and her lips curved a little at the corners. "You have three choices."

"Not that again."

She nodded. "It's the only way to know for sure."

"Aw, come on, Susana. I don't think that's such a good idea. Look at the mess it got me into before."

"That's because you rushed out and acted on incomplete information."

"And whose fault was that?"

"I admit I share some blame." She held his gaze.

"And how will you atone for your sins?" A wicked thought snuck into his head as heat crept into his loins.

"I could say I'm sorry?"

"I have a better idea."

"Oh?"

"I'll let you do a reading. By whichever method you choose."

"Good."

"But there's one condition."

She lifted a slim black brow.

"You have to do it naked."

Merely saying it aloud sent blood rushing to his extremities. Susana's eyes and mouth gaped open at the same time.

"No way." She rose to her feet, chair rasping on the floor. She picked up their plates and carried them to the sink, then started scraping leftovers vigorously into the garbage.

"Aren't you curious to see what your future holds?"

"It's really not a good idea to read one's own future. The messages can become mixed, distorted." She glanced up at him from behind the heavy curtain of hair that concealed her face while she bent over the garbage.

"Aren't you curious about my future then?"

"I have patience. The future will unfold in its own time." She dropped the lid on the garbage pail with a decisive slam.

"Come on, Susana." He spoke low, chin resting on his hands, surveying her in the dim florescent light of the tiny kitchen. His voice crept through the incense still hanging in the air. "Live dangerously for once."

She glanced at him. Curious.

"You've always done what your grandma said. You've been a good girl all these years. Aren't you in the least bit tempted to do something a little crazy?"

She turned and faced him. Placed her hands on her hips. A gesture that snugged her blouse against her breasts. Joe shifted in his chair.

"I bet you've never done a reading naked."

"Of course I haven't." She tossed her hair.

"Then maybe it's about time you did." He lifted one eyebrow very slightly.

She raised one of hers. "No touching?"

"If that's the way you want it." Excitement rippled through his muscles as he watched her contemplate the possibility. He leaned forward.

"And you..." She regarded him steadily beneath her black lashes. "Will you be naked too?"

"If you like."

He could swear he saw heat simmering behind the reflective black surface of her eyes. She was interested. She wanted to see him naked.

He ached to unzip the jeans pressing uncomfortably on the part of him that swelled with each passing second. *Easy does it, Joe.* Stealth and silence can gain more ground than heavy firepower.

"The seeing globe would be best, but it's at the shop. The palm doesn't give enough detailed information for our purposes."

"I guess that leaves the cards."

"Yes. Follow me."

Joe squeezed out from behind the table. If he had a tail it would be wagging furiously. Susana tossed her black mane again as she walked out of the room with him panting at her heels.

In the living room she opened a drawer in the bureau beneath her grandmother's hostile stare. She removed a small black box. Joe saw her hand tremble as she opened it.

His heart trembled a little, too.

Was she really going to read his future? He didn't want to know about that. He just wanted to see her naked. Was that too much to ask? Of course it was but that hadn't stopped him.

The future was going to happen anyway. He'd just as soon not know in advance what kind of crap was going to rain down on him.

He tugged his fingers through his hair. Tangled. He was still a mess. Not even dressed up for a hot date with a beautiful woman. The thought hadn't crossed his mind. In his excitement about seeing Susana again all other thoughts had shriveled temporarily out of existence.

He'd forgotten that he wasn't really a man any more. Not really human. Certainly not someone who should be staring his future in the face. *Naked.*

"You're scared, aren't you?" She spoke softly.

"Yeah," he replied honestly.

"That's okay. I'm a little scared, too."

"We can do it with clothes on if you like."

She shook her head. A flash of fierce energy filled her black stare and for a split second she reminded him of her grandmother's picture. "We'll do it naked."

Those words were enough to snap him out of a funk. "Not in here, though." He glanced up at Milos, who surprisingly had his head tucked coyly under a wing. "We don't want to shock your parrot."

"We'll do it in...in the room you slept in last night."

She swept out of the room with a determined stride.

They sat opposite each other on the bed. Still fully clothed. A single candle guttered on the windowsill.

"You first." Her serious expression should have wilted any strength left in him. Instead it only poured fuel on the flames licking around his crotch.

"Sure."

He tugged his T-shirt over his head.

She gasped and he looked up. Her mouth was round with surprise, her eyes fixed on his exposed chest.

"What are you staring at, the scar or the tattoo?" He felt oddly vulnerable with her midnight gaze burning over his torso.

"What's that scar from?"

Joe glanced down at the long white line over his belly, decorated with dots that commemorated nearly eighty stitches. "Shrapnel wound. Not too pretty, huh?"

"Does it hurt?"

"No, it's old."

"And the tattoo, it's..."

"Huge, I know. Never mix alcohol and body art."

"It's beautiful."

He looked down the eagle spreading its wings across his chest, covering his pectorals with its intricate veil of blue lines. "I had a layover in Okinawa one time. Drank a bit too much sake."

"It suits you."

"It suited who I used to be when I thought the world was my oyster."

She looked up at his face, her expression inscrutable. No doubt all those readings she did for a living gave her lots of practice at hiding her feelings. Her impersonal demeanor should have dampened his desire.

But it didn't.

"Take off your jeans." Her voice was cool, measured.

His response was equal and opposite. Heat flared inside his pants as he unbuttoned and unzipped them, an action that brought instant relief.

But the relief was only temporary. As he tugged down his shorts, exposing his erection, the heat crept up his body to heat his face.

He glanced warily at Susana. His very obvious arousal had captured her attention. She looked up, eyes wide and gleaming.

"It's big."

Joe released a quick burst of laughter. The way she stared you'd think she'd never seen one before.

Which, now that he thought about it, was a distinct possibility.

An intriguing possibility.

He settled into a comfortable position, suddenly feeling that for once he might have the upper hand here.

"Your turn."

Her chest heaved as she sucked in a breath. In just a few seconds he'd get a glimpse of that chest up close and personal. The thought was so pleasing he didn't even mind that she'd instantly see the effect it had on him.

"C'mon. Fair's fair."

She licked her lips. "Okay." She unbuttoned the neck of her blouse. Slowly, watching her hands, she slid the hem of her shirt from the waistband of her skirt.

Breathe, Joe, breathe.

Their eyes met for a split second before she lifted the shirt up over her head, pulled her arms out of the sleeves, and tossed it to the floor.

Sweet Jesus.

Full, heavy and creamy golden, her breasts shoved all other thoughts from his mind. Blushing nipples peeked out behind shiny black hair as she leaned forward and reached her arms back to unfasten the waist of her skirt. She slid the voluminous garment down the length of her legs, revealing them slowly. Long, lean, pale from a lifetime's concealment, yet muscled and shapely. Joe squashed a primitive howl that threatened to rip from his throat.

As her skirt slid to the floor, only her underwear remained. Dark briefs that rose to her impossibly slim waist. She snuck a slender finger in the waistband, then glanced up at him shyly.

He nodded.

Her hair fell to cover her face as she lifted herself and slipped the final piece of clothing down past her rosy knees, her pink-soled feet.

Naked.

Joe's body throbbed with anticipation. Of what? He couldn't touch her. He knew she wouldn't touch him.

Or would she?

She shifted awkwardly, tucking her legs under her, and Joe fought to avert his eyes from the mysterious triangle of black hair below her belly button. Struggled to keep his dignity.

She picked up the box she'd brought in from the living room and opened the lid again. Lifted out a black silk-wrapped parcel.

"The cards," she murmured, glancing up.

A pinprick of anxiety pierced Joe's fog of arousal.

Carefully, she lifted the corners of the black silk, peeling them back to reveal a deck of ordinary playing cards.

"We'll do a very simple reading." Her voice was low, calm. Two spots of color high on her cheeks the only sign this was not an ordinary day's work for Susana.

"We'll ask about only one subject."

Joe swallowed, the muscles of his gut suddenly tight.

She raised her eyes, black and unreadable. "Love."

6

Susana cut the cards and shuffled them gently, taking care not to disturb the energy in them. They'd been her grandmother's favorite set. The memory of her grandmother suddenly clung around her, almost pushing the breath from her lungs. What on earth would Granna think about her sitting here naked with a strange man?

Her fingers trembled and she struggled not to drop the cards. This was all a big mistake. Joe had offered for them to keep their clothes on. Her demand had stripped them both bare. What kind of girl actually *wanted* to see a man's naked body?

The kind of girl she'd always turned up her nose at. Who she'd felt sorry for, even as she felt sorry for herself for being different.

She blew out a soft breath, keeping her eyes low, away from the awesome spectacle of Joe's naked body.

A glorious body, beautiful and masculine. Everything about it big—broad shoulders, powerful limbs thick with muscle, the magnificent eagle tattoo spreading its wings across his chest. The long white scar slashing across his hard, flat belly.

And his...

Better not to think about that. She drew in a surreptitious breath, trying to keep her cool.

Or what was left of it.

The cards. That's why you're here. Focus on the cards.

Odd how being naked in front of this man didn't make her feel ashamed. He sat there quietly, patiently—anxious, she could tell. Anxious because he believed in her powers. She knew whether someone sat ready to listen, or whether they itched to dismiss her as a fake.

She sneaked a glance up at Joe as she prepared to spread the cards. He forced a quick smile, trying to put her at ease. She could tell he was a kind man, or had been once. Like he said, neither of them knew who he'd become.

But that was beside the point.

Her business was the reading at hand. Love.

Her fingers tingled with anticipation and apprehension. She had something at stake here too. She wanted to know the future of Joe's love life.

Because she wondered... *It's not your place to speculate.* No good came of trying to predict your own destiny, any decent seer knew that.

She laid three cards face-up between them on the white bedspread, announcing as she did, "Past, present, future."

Uh-oh.

As her mind quickly calculated the meanings she was tempted to gather them up and make an excuse and start again. Sometimes stray vibrations produced a reading that didn't accurately reflect the question at hand. It was perfectly acceptable to scratch a reading and start over.

She looked at Joe, who glanced up at her, eager, nervous. And she couldn't lie to him.

"The first card is the queen of clubs."

"I can see that."

"It stands for a woman."

"Aha." He shifted and she could almost hear the tension crackling through his body. He expected her to talk about his past, about the woman who'd... Well, she had no idea what that woman had done to him.

But the cards spoke of a different woman.

"The card signifies fire and art. Power and passion." She looked up at him.

"Not sure that describes my ex too well. Greed and deceit would be more accurate." She could see him relaxing. Because he'd dismissed the reading out of hand. He no longer believed her.

And maybe that was for the best.

She paused, tore her eyes from his and placed her hand lightly over the card. The vibrations hummed in her fingertips. The power. "This is the card my grandmother used in readings to signify..." The word caught in her throat.

Power and passion, the force of her gift.

"What?" Joe looked curious. No longer nervous now he didn't take the process seriously. His eyes drifted to her breasts, and her nipples tightened.

How much of herself should she bare? "She used it to signify me."

Joe's eyes snapped back to her face. "You?"

She nodded. "Fire and art, the fire of the life force, and the art to read and interpret it."

"But why would it show you in my past? We don't have a past. Unless you count that one reading." His forehead creased in perplexity.

"Perhaps it refers to that night. To the reading that set you on a course."

"The wrong course." His eyes narrowed and she could hear the edge in his voice. He hadn't quite forgiven her.

"Again you're jumping to conclusions."

"Oh?" He cocked an eyebrow.

"Perhaps it was the right course."

"Yeah, right. I guess I was supposed to get my heart ripped out of my chest and tossed in the trash." He looked away into the darkened room, the candlelight flickering over his hard, handsome features.

"But where did that course bring you?" She cautioned herself to go slow. To ask more questions than she answered.

"To the pit of hell." He hissed the words through almost closed lips, staring at the dark floor.

"And then where?"

He lifted his head, and his eyes crept back to meet hers. "Here."

She didn't speak. She'd learned over the years to provide the facts and let the seeker draw their own conclusions. It took time and patience and wasn't good for business. But it was good for the seeker.

"Hmph." He lifted a hand and rubbed his opposite bicep. "Okay... So what does the next card say, the Present?"

A shimmer of adrenaline stung her as she licked her lips, preparing to part with the words.

"The six of hearts. It's a good card. It speaks of kindness, of the beginning of a new relationship." She kept her eyes firmly focused on the card, the six red hearts almost seeming to beat in the flickering candlelight. "Or blessings on an old one."

"Or all of the above?" Joe's eyes searched her face.

"Possibly." She stilled her tongue.

He nodded. "You've been kind to me. Given me a place to sleep, made me breakfast. We have an old relationship in that I remembered you and came back—for whatever reason." He paused, blinked, his gaze darting from eye to eye. "I don't know why I came back, I honestly don't. Something pulled me there."

Fate.

She didn't say it though. Let him draw his own conclusions. It was safer, for him anyway.

"And the beginnings of a new relationship." His face brightened, almost glowing in the golden light from the single flame.

He held his hand out and she took it. Warm and firm. Pleasure stirred in her as she watched a smile spread across his mouth and light his harsh features.

She kept her eyes firmly fixed on his face, fighting the urge to let them wander over his thick muscles, down the trail of black hair that snaked over his belly to his...

He'd just broken the no-touching rule.

She tugged at her hand, trying to pull it back.

"Do you really want to do that?"

"No," she admitted. She wanted to touch him. To hold him, even. Her eyes dropped to the eagle spreading its wings over his broad chest, proud head held high.

Excitement rustled inside her at the thought of spreading her own wings. Of flying free.

Free of the bounds of tradition and obligation. Free of the "gift" that held her in bondage. Free of her grandmother's rules and restrictions. To be an ordinary girl, with an ordinary life.

With a man.

Joe bent his head and she instinctively rose to meet him. His lips brushed her cheek, warm breath caressing her. He slid toward her, crushing the cards as his arms closed around her shoulders.

Her hands slid under his armpits and stretched to reach around his thick torso. "Oh, Joe." The words escaped her as she let herself fall into his embrace. So solid, warm and steady.

And more.

Joe kissed her ear, his tongue flicking gently over her earlobe to send a shudder that rippled to her toes. As her nipples hardened they grazed the firm muscle of his chest. She gasped at the sensation, fleeting yet so intense.

Then she remembered the third card.

The five of diamonds. A card of warning.

Joe's finger skated up her spine as goose bumps sprang up on her arms and breasts. His hand dove into her hair, fingers tangling behind her neck as he cupped her head and tipped it back.

Her fingers stiffened, ready to push him back, to give him the warning. But his mouth stole her breath and her resolve.

As his tongue plunged in she softened in his arms. He'd come to her, come *for* her. He wanted her.

She didn't know what exactly he wanted. Not a lifetime of love. He wanted her body. Her breasts. One broad hand covered her right breast, chafing the nipple with his thumb. Already creating tremors, spasms in muscles she never knew she had.

What was she doing?

She knew. She'd been there in her dream. Felt the ghostly foreshadowing of these powerful sensations, now far more intense in reality than in imagination.

He tugged her to him, his hard arousal pushing bluntly against her belly. The fierce edge of his need tangible in the force of his kiss, in the pressure of his fingertips on her skin.

And she felt her own need growing within her like a dark force. Twenty-three years old and until Joe she'd never known the touch of a man. Never had a rough cheek brush against hers, or known the demand of a strong embrace.

His hands slid down her back, grazing the skin in a gentle caress, sending shivers of longing that penetrated to her heart.

She moaned as he cupped her buttocks and pulled her up against him, crushing her breasts against his chest, burying them in the eagle's wings. Her belly rubbed against his, over the scar that had healed but would never disappear.

She knew his scars went beyond the visible. She'd seen the pain in his eyes, black as they were, like hers. She'd looked past the reflective onyx surface to the soul within, and his was wounded. Possibly in a way that would never heal.

He wasn't hers to keep, and she knew that.

Tonight you shall meet the woman you are destined to spend your life with. Her own words taunted her.

What if she'd acted differently then? If she'd claimed the life presented in the crystal ball? If she'd reached out to him?

But he was *gadjo*—non-gypsy, unclean and off limits. And she was spoken for—by tradition, by pride, by family.

What she did now was wrong. All wrong.

She shoved her fingers roughly into his hair, tugged on it. Her body hummed with strange messages, contradictory songs of warning and desire, and she couldn't understand them. Didn't want to.

And Joe's hand slid under their bellies and between

her legs. His fingers already wet with evidence of her longing.

Heat softened her limbs, melting her as desire threatened to quash all rational thought. But as his hand dove into the hot, damp space between her legs, she knew they were coming close to the point of no return.

"Stop."

Instantly he stopped. Withdrew his hand from between her thighs. Opened his eyes.

His arousal throbbed once against her belly, startling her. Then he pulled away, leaving nothing but empty air touching her skin. Leaving the cards crumpled and disarranged on the bedspread.

He knelt before her, fiercely aroused yet holding himself back. Respecting her.

She hesitated, kneeling, naked and glowing with arousal. Muscles pulsed, soft tissues throbbed, craving his touch.

"I've never done this before."

"That's okay. We can take it slow." She watched his Adam's apple bob as he swallowed. "Or stop."

A muscle twitched in his cheek.

She should stop. This was crazy.

Did she really want to risk losing her powers? To give up the gift that set her apart?

Joe held out his hand to her, palm up. She took it.

"It's okay to be nervous. We can just hold each other."

Heat from his palm sizzled against hers. The vibrations stronger than anything she'd ever felt from the cards or the seeing globe.

The energy gathering between them threatened to dwarf the powers she'd cultivated and nurtured, that she'd built her whole life around.

But how could she live if she no longer had the ability to read fortunes? Could she fake it?

Or should she fake it now? Tell him she'd changed her mind. That she wasn't interested. Invoke the rules.

Joe settled back onto his haunches, squeezed her hand. She could see his desire still rigid and unyielding, waiting and hoping.

And she hadn't warned him about the third card. Again she held secrets close to her chest, guarding her advantage.

But this time her chest was bare. Her breasts exposed, nipples tight and flushed with arousal. She owed him the truth. This time at least she wouldn't deny him that.

"The third card..." She paused, tossed her hair behind her back, then regretted it as she realized she'd left her breasts totally uncovered. Joe's eyes dropped to them.

Again she felt the power she wielded. Not just psychic power but the power of a woman, the power to give or to withhold.

Joe's black eyes rose to meet hers.

"The third card...?" he repeated, a question in his voice.

"It's not a good card." She swallowed.

"No." He blinked. "I didn't suppose it would be."

She saw the glow in his eyes dim a little, the hopeful optimism lighting his features wither. And that hurt her heart.

"It's just a card."

"What exactly is the meaning?"

"It speaks of cowardice, rumor, possible betrayal... It's a card of warning."

"Been there, done that. Are you going to betray me,

Susana?"

"I don't know."

"At least you're honest."

He squeezed her hand gently. Looked at her with eyes soft and brown in the shifting candlelight.

"I don't know what the future holds, Joe."

"So you're a fake?" He said it warmly, tilting his head to one side. It occurred to her that he wanted her to be a fake. Didn't mind if she was ordinary. And at that moment she wished she were.

"No, I'm not a fake. My powers are real, but they are limited. I can see possibilities, potential problems, but I can never predict a clear outcome."

"Do you tell your clients that?"

"Sometimes."

"You didn't tell me that ten years ago. You spoke with such assurance."

"I was young. I've learned a lot since then. Learned to use my readings to guide people into making their own decisions."

"Like a psychologist, helping them figure out their lives?"

"Yes." She held his hand firm. "You understand. That's exactly how I see my work."

Her relatives laughed at her grand ideas about helping people. They were happy to pocket the money and send the punters on their way with a smile on their face. A dose of hope and a fistful of questions to keep them coming back. But that wasn't satisfying to her.

"You're helping me right now." One side of Joe's mouth lifted into the beginnings of a smile.

"Oh?"

"The past and future may be a bit cockeyed, but I'm enjoying the present very much."

His throaty voice roamed though the air, rich with suggestion as his eyes drifted slowly down over her neck, her breasts and belly, to her thighs.

He released his grip on her hand and let one finger trail over the inside of her wrist, over her palm. She shuddered at the sensation. "Perhaps I should read your future." He glanced up, his eyes black again, shimmering with intrigue. "I see you trying something new...something different. Something a little risky. And a lot pleasurable."

As he spoke his fingertip traced a circle over her palm. Then he lifted her hand and covered her palm with his hot, wet mouth. Licked along her heart line, along her life line, along the line representing the head she was in grave danger of losing.

"You're a virgin, aren't you?" He lifted an eyebrow and looked at her.

"Yes," she admitted quietly.

"And do you wish to remain one?" He spoke formally, as if interviewing her. But his voice emerged low, husky and seductive.

"I don't know." She shifted again, heat and wet uncomfortable between her legs. She craved this man. Craved everything about him. His big hard body, his handsome scarred face, his pain-filled eyes. She kept her gaze fixed on the blue ink scrawled over his torso, avoiding the obvious sign of his fierce arousal beneath it.

"You should stay a virgin."

Even as he said it she knew he didn't mean it. His hand skimmed along her arm, traced the curve of her armpit and slid down to glide along the underside of her bare breast. The sensation of fingertips on the sensitive skin made her suck in a breath.

"You've saved yourself until now. You should wait

until the right man comes along."

But what if you are the right man?

She didn't say the question aloud, but he heard it anyway.

"I can't offer you anything beyond a night of pleasure. I know I can offer you that." His eyes narrowed. "Sexual pleasure is one area of life where I know I won't disappoint. Where I won't be disappointed. I guess that's why it beckons me now, when there's nothing else I can count on."

She dropped her eyes to the hand caressing her breast, then back up to meet his steady gaze. "If you think I should wait, why are you still touching me? You're breaking the rules." Her voice emerged as a whisper, breathless with want. And with fear. Fear of her own aching need.

"It's the beast inside me. The crazy, dangerous part that keeps me awake at nights when everyone else is sleeping. The beast wants you."

"And the honorable man?"

"He wants you, too."

He cupped her breast and lifted it slightly. Lowered his lips and kissed her nipple. Then gently let go and withdrew his hand.

"But the honorable man can rein himself in, tug the beast back and shove him in his cage." Candlelight flashed in his eyes as he lifted his head. "If that's what you want."

"Why do you want me?"

"Because you're a beautiful girl."

"Is it that simple?"

"There's nothing simple about it. It's why we're here. The future of humanity depends upon a man wanting a woman."

"Or a woman wanting a man."

She wasn't a girl any more. She'd become a woman, ready to claim the pleasures of a woman.

She let her eyes drift down to explore the man she wanted. His body still hard, rigid and humming with barely contained aggression—but now desire drove him, not anger. His muscles steady and unmoving as she roved over his tan skin with her mind.

She didn't read auras, not even as an amateur, but she could feel the halo of warm color around him, feel the pull as every cell in his body murmured, *come to me, take me, hold me.*

Love me.

Even just for one night.

"I don't have protection," she whispered, afraid to hear her voice in the still night air.

"Don't worry, I have some."

He climbed off the bed and found his jeans where they lay crumpled on the floor. He fished in a pocket and pulled out a blue packet. Still rock hard, he climbed back on the bed and held it out to her.

She took the packet. Small and square, covered with tiny print.

"Why did you buy this when we'd agreed you wouldn't touch me?"

"Men are hopeful creatures." His lips curved in a shy smile.

Susana fingered the packet. He knew she was a virgin. He offered her nothing beyond tonight. He planned to take her innocence and disappear over the horizon.

At least you're honest.

There were no lies between them. No false promises.

"I don't know how to put it on."

He held out his hand and she placed the packet in it. He ripped it open. She caught her breath and held it, biting her lip hard.

"Are you sure?"

She nodded.

She wasn't sure of anything at all except that she wanted Joe inside her. Wanted to feel him filling up the empty spaces she'd carried around for so long. Wanted to take that first big step on the road to building her own life.

And if she woke up without her powers, so be it.

He sheathed the impressive length of his erection and tossed the packet aside.

"Let me make sure you're ready." His voice was throaty with barely controlled passion. He pushed her gently back until she lay on the bed, skin glowing gold in the reflected candlelight.

Joe crawled over her, on all fours, like a hungry predator ready to claim her. The musky male scent of him filled her nostrils.

She reached up and touched his face with her hand as he brought a probing finger between her legs.

"You're ready, all right."

She could feel her own slickness, her muscles throbbing and aching with the urge to have him moving inside her.

He leaned forward to kiss her face, his rough cheek brushing against hers, a hint of the raw maleness ready to fill her.

"I'm glad you finished the reading," he murmured, his lips hotly moving over her ear. "Forewarned is forearmed."

She could feel his smile against her cheek as the tip of his penis danced over her sensitive flesh. She heard a little moan escape her lips.

"I won't betray you," she whispered. No matter what else, she could promise him that.

"You won't lie to me?"

"Never." Her words were almost lost in the heat of his mouth as it claimed hers. He licked her lips, then pulled back just one almost unbearable inch.

She rocked her hips into him, begging him to enter, to bury himself in her.

"Tomorrow you can do a new reading for me and see if my fate has changed." His low voice barely penetrated the thick fog of arousal clouding her mind. "Will you?"

"Umm..." words danced just outside her consciousness. She didn't want to think about tomorrow.

But she'd promised not to lie to him.

"I may not be able to," she breathed.

"Why?" he whispered, his smile pressing against her cheek.

At least you're honest.

"Because I may lose my powers along with my virginity."

"What?" He tugged back, and cool night air assaulted her cheek where his lips had breathed so hotly just a second ago.

She moaned and writhed against him. She didn't want to think about her powers, or anything else but Joe's big body moving inside hers.

She groped for words to answer him. "That's what usually happens."

Goose bumps rose over her skin as he pulled further away from her. Eyes still closed, she groped the air with her hands, reaching for him.

"Susana, you can't be serious..." The grave tone of his

voice tugged her eyes open. "You can't... I can't..."

"Please." The pleading sound of her own voice echoed the pulsing throb of desperate need still pounding through her body. Twenty-three years of longing, pent up and ready to break free.

"I can't, Susana. I can't take that from you. I have nothing to offer you."

He leaped off the bed and strode to the far wall. She could make out the lines of his body in the dim shadows cast by the single candle.

"I don't care about my powers. I've been a prisoner of them my whole life." She sat up on the bed. "I want to be free."

"I can't do it." He turned to her. Shadows hid his face. "I can't take responsibility for you losing your gift. You told me to keep my hands off you. You wanted me to keep my distance, and I didn't."

"That was my decision, too."

"No. I led you to it. You're aroused. You're not thinking straight."

She shook her head, hair flying, confused thoughts tumbling around in her mind. "I want you, Joe."

"And I want you, too, Susana. But not at such a high cost."

"But the cost is to me, not you."

"I know. And you're young. You'll live to regret it. And I won't take the blame, not any more."

He strode across the room and snatched his jeans off the floor, tugging them on roughly. "You should have told me, Susana."

"I did tell you." She swallowed, tears welling up in her throat and under her eyelids. "I did tell you, and I wish I hadn't."

"Don't cry." His balled up T-shirt gathered in one

hand, he sat on the bed.

"Why not?" Her words emerged as a sob. "Why won't anyone let me make my own decisions about my life?"

"Come here." He eased toward her on the bed and wrapped his arms around her. Her tears wet the skin of his shoulder as she buried her face in it. "If you really want to...make love, we'll do it. But I want it to be a decision you make in the cold light of day."

She looked up at him, vision blurred with tears. A broad thumb stroked the wetness from her cheek.

"If you think about it, truly think about it, and you still want to... Come find me tomorrow evening. I'll write down the address of my new apartment. If you don't come, I'll understand that too."

She couldn't find any words to reply so she simply nodded, tears dripping onto her bare breasts, as he rose off the bed, picked up his shoes and left.

As the door closed behind him she swiped at her tears with a shaking hand. She was tired of people telling her what to do. She'd done everything Granna said for twenty-three years. It was time to take charge of her own life.

She climbed off the bed, blew out the candle and propped her elbows on the windowsill. She waited for him to write his note, let himself out of the apartment and descend the stairs.

Then she watched as he emerged from the building, strode diagonally across the street and took off up the sidewalk as if the hounds of hell snapped at his heels.

7

Joe opened the massive sliding door to his loft apartment with a huge smile.

"Come in."

He knew she'd come. She could see it right away. Suddenly Susana felt ashamed that she'd had second thoughts and almost backed out.

He gestured for her to step over the threshold. As she did she heard piano music tinkling in the background. Little notes of fear jingled inside her.

"Wow." The apartment was stunning. Huge, with high ceilings and gleaming wood floors. A wall of windows looked out over the Hudson River, gray water still visible in the dusk, lights gleaming on the opposite bank.

"I've been busy. I rented the place unfurnished."

She looked around and wanted to laugh. It still looked unfurnished—no rugs on the floor or pictures on the white walls. Just a table, set for two, with two chairs. And the tiny silver stereo system on the floor in a corner of the room.

"There's a bed, too," he said softly.

Susana bit her lip.

A delicious aroma drew her attention to the kitchen

open to the big living room. Two pots steamed on a huge stove surrounded by pale stone countertops.

"Arroz con pollo."

"What's that?"

"Chicken and rice. My dad's recipe."

"Smells good."

Pretty confident of him to start cooking before she showed up. They hadn't agreed on a time. But she'd known when to come.

"Would you like something to drink?"

"Sure."

"Wine?" Joe gestured at a bottle, already uncorked, sitting on the granite counter.

"Okay." Just a sip, she promised herself. No sense getting tipsy. She wanted to savor every single minute of this adventure with all her senses fully awake.

She watched as Joe poured red wine into two large wineglasses. He'd combed his hair back neatly from his handsome face, tan cheeks shaved clean. His light blue shirt looked new, the creases from the packaging precise and crisp.

"You look different."

"I clean up nice, huh?" He smiled and walked toward her with a glass of wine.

She nodded and took the glass from him, then smiled as she surveyed his bottom half. Faded jeans and bare feet.

He shrugged. "I'm still me. At least my top half looks pretty. To good fortune." He lifted his glass and clinked it against hers.

"Good fortune." She repeated and took a sip. The fruity liquid tickled her tongue, and she shivered, all on edge with excitement, anticipation and anxiety.

"You look different too."

She realized his eyes hadn't left her face until now. She tucked her hair behind her ear as his gaze wandered down over the new outfit she'd bought with so much trepidation that afternoon.

She'd wanted to wear jeans, but she'd tried them on and known she'd feel naked walking down the streets with the intimate curves of her thighs and backside, her crotch, on display to everyone.

She'd bought a dress, with a neckline that revealed her collarbone. The knee-length hem was demure by modern standards but shockingly risqué for Susana. The deep, plum shade flattered her complexion and brought out the color in her lips and cheeks.

"What do you think?" She smoothed the fabric of her skirt, suddenly self-conscious, like a kid playing dress-up.

"Very sophisticated. You look dazzlingly beautiful. But then you always do." Joe's dark eyes rested warmly on her face as he took a sip of his wine.

Susana's face heated at the unfamiliar compliment. She'd heard her share of bloated flattery from drunken clients, but that didn't mean anything. The only references to her looks from people she knew were entreaties to cover herself up, hide herself from the prying eyes of strangers, unless she wanted to end up like trampy cousin Sonya.

Or like her mother.

She took another sip of the dark liquid.

"You ready to eat?"

"Sure."

Joe had lit a candle at the table and the flame guttered as Susana lowered herself carefully into her seat. Her skirt slid up to reveal half her bare thighs and she was glad the table hid the bold display. Odd really, when she'd sat before him last night without a stitch on and not even felt shy.

Joe brought over two steaming plates of fragrant chicken and rice with black beans, then settled into the seat in front of her.

"My dad was from Cuba. This was his favorite dish." Joe's smiling face shone, so astonishingly different from the haggard, haunted countenance she'd seen in the shop two days ago. Almost unrecognizable.

Could she take credit for the transformation? Or did all men look like that when they thought they were going to get laid?

She shoved her napkin down into her lap, as if it could smother the flames of heat and embarrassment leaping under her new dress.

She'd promised and now she'd have to deliver.

"Go ahead, dig in." He led the way, forking chicken into his smiling mouth.

Susana arranged some chicken on her fork and lifted it cautiously. This was, what—the third meal they'd eaten together? Why did she feel so self-conscious?

The aromatic chicken filled her taste buds with its savory flavors. "This is great."

"Thanks. I bet you didn't think I could cook."

"You're right." Embarrassment forgotten, she ate more of the delicious food.

"My dad was a fantastic cook. It's what he did for a living. My mom too, she came from Italy and had cooking in her blood, she said. Even on their days off they'd spend all day in the kitchen, so I grew up eating well."

"Lucky you."

"Yeah," he nodded thoughtfully. "I was lucky. I had a happy childhood."

A shadow darted across his features and his eyes dropped to his plate as he gathered another mouthful of food.

"I could see that when you came into the shop ten years ago. You glowed with high spirits." She hesitated for a second before admitting the truth. "It was very attractive."

"High spirits, huh?" He shook his head, chuckling. "Naïve dumbass ignorance is probably a better description. I'm all wised up now, though." He looked away and took a quick swig of his wine.

"What happened, Joe? With your wife."

He didn't look up. Her stomach tightened. She would have liked to just enjoy the delicious meal, but suddenly Joe's past hung between them like a knife, cutting through casual conversation.

"She dumped me. She promised me for better or for worse..." He shook his head. "But I guess she wasn't up for the worse."

"You feel a sense of betrayal."

"Wouldn't you? Marriage is for life. That's the whole point of it. I provided for her, took care of her. Hell, I loved her. She was my wife." He seized his glass and took a swig of wine, avoiding her gaze.

"I'm sorry she hurt you."

"Me too."

"The 'worse' you mentioned. Does that have anything to do with your scars?"

"Sure does. But trust me, you don't want to know." He shoved a forkful of food in his mouth and chewed it.

"Sometimes it helps to talk about what's troubling you. I can see the past still haunts you."

"You can, can you?" His eyes met hers, suddenly hard. "I bet you can read all about my sorry existence right in the palm of my hand." He slammed a hand, palm up, down on the table.

Susana forced herself not to read the lines. Not that they would have told her much anyway. He balled his hand into a fist and withdrew it.

"Why did your grandmother raise you?" His black eyes narrowed as he asked the question. "What happened to your parents?"

An assault—as a form of defense. He didn't want to talk about his own past so he'd picked up an obviously painful chunk of hers and hurled it at her.

She grasped her wineglass and raised it to her lips. Her hand slipped and the glass clinked against her teeth, making her blink. She put the glass down. Surely after all these years she should be able to talk about this.

But she never had.

It was taboo, a dirty secret that contaminated all who knew it, most of all her.

She drew in a ragged breath.

"Hey, I'm sorry," Joe reached a hand across the table. "If you don't want to talk about it, that's okay. Believe me, I know how that goes."

She placed her hand in his, and he closed his fingers around it, stroking the back of her hand with his thumb. Sparks of warmth tickled her skin where he chafed it. Why did his touch feel so good? Already she was relaxing.

Already she found herself wanting to tell him.

"My dad wasn't Rom. He worked in a bakery where my mom went to buy bread. They started meeting each other secretly." She paused, the forbidden words dancing around her. "I only know this tenth hand, mind you, since they died when I was a baby."

"Did they get married?"

"No. They never married, but she got pregnant." Susana looked at their hands intertwined on the table. They fit together so well. Suddenly she wondered if her mother ever had that same thought as she held hands with her *gadjo* lover.

The idea shocked her and made tears spring to her throat.

Her mother's name was never mentioned. It was unclean.

"The shame of her pregnancy made my grandfather cast her out, so she went to live with her lover."

"What was his name?"

"I don't know."

"But you have his last name, right?"

She shook her head. "My grandmother gave her name when she took me in. She wanted to forget my *gadjo* heritage."

"Damn."

"My mother's name was Marianna." The word burned her tongue, as if she cursed herself by saying it. But that bitter, frightening sting was also the taste of freedom. "She was only nineteen when she died." She swallowed back the hot lump forming in her throat.

"What happened?"

"They were both shot dead one night."

"By your family?"

"No!"

Fear curled Susana's hand into a fist as she stared at Joe. *Was it possible?* The idea had never occurred to her. And she didn't want to consider it.

"They said my father got mixed up in a drug deal. I don't know any more than that. I was in the apartment when they were shot. Everyone called it a miracle I wasn't hurt."

"I bet your childhood wasn't so easy." He tightened his protective grip on her hand.

She avoided his eyes, trying to shrug off the unfamiliar wave of emotion tugging at her. She'd grown practiced at keeping her feelings under wraps, concealing them so carefully from everyone that she'd learned how to hide them even from herself.

"Did the family accept you, even though you're only half gypsy?"

She nodded. "Mostly. The Rom look after their own. There was always whispering, backbiting, but my grandmother wouldn't hear anything said against me. And when they realized I had the gift..."

She blew out a breath. The gift had saved her life in a way. Transformed her from a tolerated pariah into a proudly claimed member of the family.

And now she was going to give it up? Throw her powers away for one night with a handsome *gadjo*? Her fingers cooled inside his grasp.

"The gift is your ability to read fortunes?" Joe lifted a dark eyebrow.

"More than that. Anyone can read fortunes if they learn the language of the cards, of the palm. It's the third eye, the ability to see what lies beyond the present..." She pulled her hand from his, grabbed her wineglass and took a quick swig.

The liquid blasted her mouth with its bittersweet shock. She put the glass down and tossed her head.

"It's never done me any good. What's the point of seeing the future? Better just to meet it when you get there."

"Your family is going to have a fit if you lose your powers."

"No, they won't. They won't even know. I can fake it."

"No you can't." Joe leaned forward, eyes narrowed, glittering in the candlelight. "I don't know you well, but I know you're no faker. You'd rather eat glass than tell a lie."

"Oh yeah? Like you said, you don't know me so well." She narrowed her own eyes, matching his intense stare, meeting him blow for blow.

Of course he was right, but there was no need to let him know that.

She sat back in her chair, lifting her shoulders and trying to show a confidence she didn't feel. "I'm sick of sitting in a dusty storefront telling fortunes all day."

"What do you want to do?"

She blinked. She'd never spoken aloud about her dream. It was her secret. Once she put it into words she could be mocked, laughed at, pitied.

She fingered her wineglass. "I'd like to be a psychologist." Spoken out loud it sounded pretentious. She waved her hand in the air as if she could erase the words. She'd removed her bracelets and the lack of expected sound startled her, increasing her embarrassment.

Joe's eyebrow lifted. "That sounds like a great idea. Why not?"

"I didn't even finish high school."

Sorry Susana, we need you to start earning.

"So? You can get a GED, go to college."

Her mouth twitched. That was her plan. The one she'd turned over in her mind night after night alone in her bed. Her impossible dream.

To hear it coming out of someone else's mouth made it sound just a little bit possible.

"Do you really think I can?"

"Of course." Joe looked perplexed, as if he couldn't understand why she wasn't doing it already.

"I've already started," she said shyly. Toying with her fork. "After Granna died, I sent away for the GED materials. I think I'm ready to take the test."

"Go, Susana." He lifted his glass, and she met it with hers. They swallowed wine together, and as the ruby liquid dazzled her throat, Joe's eyes danced over her face, shining.

His handsome features seemed lit from inside tonight, his tanned skin glowing with life and health. A flash of humor sparkled in the dark depths of his eyes as he lifted his chin.

"Wait a minute here. I'm part of your big plan, aren't I?"

"What?" A cool flash of adrenaline darted through her. Did he think she wanted more than one night? *Did she?*

"I have a funny feeling you're just itching to get rid of those powers of yours. Like you've been depending on them for so long they've become a bad habit. And if you get rid of them, you'll be halfway to building a new life."

She tossed her head, flicking her hair behind her shoulders. "Maybe."

"I've never been anyone's key to freedom before." His broad shoulders leaned against the back of his chair as his eyes drifted over her face, down to the plunging neckline of her dress. "I think I like it."

Susana's chest heated under the searing stare he aimed at it. Bad manners. But she liked it. She shifted a little, her breasts moving inside her dress, nipples rubbing against the stiff fabric.

"You're still not wearing a bra, are you?"

"No. I've never worn one."

"I hope you never do. Some things were meant to be free." He winked, and the crude gesture further tickled and heated her insides.

She let her gaze wander over his face, clean shaven, tanned except the pale curved scar at his eyebrow. She took in the hard line of his jaw, lifted in appraisal, and the thick sinews of his neck.

The crisp collar of his light blue shirt framed a seductive triangle of bronze skin that hinted at the powerful chest beneath it. She'd seen that chest, heavy muscle adorned with thin blue lines that spoke of his ability to endure pain.

His rolled-up sleeves revealed sturdy forearms sprinkled with dark hair. He leaned forward and placed his elbows on the table.

"We appear to be done eating."

"The food was delicious. I've never met a man who could cook."

"To be honest I hadn't cooked in a long time. Cooking is a celebration of life, and I haven't felt like celebrating anything for a while."

"And you do now?"

The wine had seeped into her brain, brightening the room, making everything shine in the soft candlelight. She didn't feel tipsy, just calmer, bolder.

"I do." A smile hovered behind his lips, not fully committing itself. "I'd like to dance with you, Susana."

"I don't know how." She shrank back in her chair, suddenly feeling like an outsider again. The tinkling piano music flowed from the speakers, mocking her. How did you dance to a bunch of tinkling notes?

"There aren't any set steps to the dance I have in mind. You make it up as you go along. Come." He rose from his chair and rounded the table. She grasped his outstretched hand and stood.

He settled one big hand in the hollow of her back, above her buttocks. His fingers trailed down over the curves, radiating heat and energy that seeped through her dress as he led her out into the big, empty room.

"I'm glad you came tonight." He slid both arms around her waist, holding her loosely, a few inches between them. He started to sway, very gently, following the ebb and flow of the piano music.

Susana stood still, too self-conscious to swing her hips, aware of the way her dress followed the shape of her body, tracing its curves.

Joe's eyes dropped to her chest as he tugged her closer, still swaying. Again she felt her nipples thrusting against the fabric, alive with sensation. Could he see her arousal through the plum colored material?

He pulled her nearer, heat swelling between them as her chest came dangerously close to bumping up against his. As his hands splayed over her back, pulling her to him, her lips parted—opening and welcoming the hot, male taste of his kiss.

Joe's low groan vibrated through their joined mouths as their tongues met. Her body softened and melted, threatening to slide right through his hands, and she grabbed his thick torso to keep her balance.

Eyes now closed, she couldn't see anything, only feel. Feelings pounded her senses—his hard muscle under her groping fingertips, his fierce mouth on hers, stealing her breath and firing her with desire and longing that thundered through her veins.

She scraped her fingers over the stiff cotton of his shirt, enjoying the ridges of muscle under it. Her hands slid down to his waistband, and lower, to cup the firm curve of his backside through the soft denim of his well-worn jeans.

Joe groaned again, abandoned to the sensation of their kiss. His hands wandered unchecked over her body, exploring her back and buttocks, squeezing and stroking. His arousal thickened in his jeans and pressed against her.

He seemed so vulnerable at that moment.

Crazy for her.

And the thought heightened her arousal, as his fingers snuck around to stroke her nipples through the fabric of her dress.

She heard herself moan, a high-pitched sound that came from somewhere she didn't know existed. Somewhere hot and wild. And crazy, too.

She tipped her pelvis, pressing into his hardness as she heard the rasp of her zipper being pulled down.

Joe broke their kiss and left her panting as he backed off a few inches and raised his hands to her shoulders. He tugged gently at her dress and it fell forward into his hands.

Susana opened her eyes, and even the candlelight shone blindingly bright. Joe's face was taut with concentration, unself-conscious, open mouthed, as he took his time removing her arms from the sleeves of her dress.

Down it fell, sliding along her legs to the floor. He took her hand like a gallant knight leading her around a puddle as he assisted her in stepping out of it.

She hadn't worn any underwear.

"Damn." The single word hissed from Joe's lips as he let his eyes wander shamelessly over her naked body. His admiring gaze heated her skin like a caress.

Her hands moved without her permission. Rising to

unbutton Joe's crisp new shirt and yank down the zipper on his jeans. Joe stood still, watching through narrowed eyes as she pushed his shirt back over his shoulders, baring his tattooed chest and upper arms.

On instinct she licked each of his nipples once, leaving them wet and gleaming. She glanced up to see his face contorted with desire, the angular cut of his cheekbones and chin sharpened by the tension.

Tension in the air. Tension in their bodies.

He tugged his shirt off the rest of the way while she pushed his jeans and underwear down the length of his muscled thighs, enjoying the prickle of wiry masculine hair that dusted them.

He stepped out of his jeans, movements jerky and rigid, barely controlled. Her blood heated to boiling point at the sight of his beautiful, powerful body standing naked before her.

The music stopped and the only sound was the hum of the fridge and the hum of the blood in her head.

"There's no turning back now," Joe whispered, his breath hot on her ear.

"I don't want to turn back," she replied, her voice oddly calm. Her resolve was total. Tonight she would become a woman.

The past was just that, the past.

And the future was nobody's business.

8

Joe took her by the hand, boyish, almost shy as he led her to the bedroom door.

"I bought the bed this morning. Had to raise hell to get it delivered today." He shot her a smile, and she smiled back and squeezed his hand.

A single lit candle glowed from the corner of the room. Their shadows loomed over the far wall as they walked silently to the bed.

The big white rectangle with its single flimsy sheet looked intimidating as the uncharted territory on an old map. *Here there be dragons.*

Joe climbed on first, a little awkward, still holding her hand as he slid across the mattress. She put one knee on the bed, sank in and almost lost her balance, then caught herself with her free hand.

He pulled her to him, settling her sideways between his legs. His erection tickled her belly as his lips played over her ear.

"Before we make love, I'm going to get you very, very ready."

She shivered, from the hot breath on her ear and the mix of apprehension and eagerness bubbling inside her.

"Lie down."

She obeyed, stretching herself out on the cool sheet, head back on a pillow.

His warm fingers traced a circle on her belly. The muscle contracted, responding to his touch, and a surge of heat shimmered under his fingers.

Gently, he pried her legs apart with his hands and climbed between them. He looked up at her, black eyes shining as his mouth followed his fingers to her belly, lips tracing the circle, breath caressing the tender skin. Susana writhed with pleasure.

His lips trailed lower, into the dark hair that hid her sex. The shock of his cool tongue on her swollen flesh made her gasp. As he settled his mouth over her, enveloping her, her eyes slid shut and she gave herself over to the sheer sensation.

Her fingers twined into his hair as his tongue fueled a series of tiny explosions deep inside her. Her nerves tangled and she forgot where she ended and he began.

His hands roamed over her warm skin, teasing the flesh of her thighs and hips, cupping her breasts, stroking her skin as she moaned. And all the while, his hot mouth licked and sucked her into a state of almost unbearable arousal.

He pulled away softly, then gave one last lick, causing her to throb in response.

"Please..." she whispered, her voice thick with need. "I'm ready."

She opened her eyes, and the tender look on his face tripped her heart. Dark eyes wide with desire and eager anticipation. He smiled at her. "I think you are."

He sheathed himself with a condom and crawled over her gingerly, his body heat rising to meet her. With one warm, tender finger, he parted her, readying her for the penetration.

Instinctive muscles tightened, desire suddenly overcome by fear.

"Just relax, take it easy," he whispered. "I'll take care of you."

She blew out a breath. He rubbed her sex gently until she softened again, easing under his caress. Then he slowly began to enter the wet warmth.

Susana writhed, wanting him inside her.

She heard his chuckle in her ear. "Impatient, aren't you?"

A soft groan was her only response. Her fingers played over his spine as he arched his back and deepened the penetration another inch.

"Oh." The sound escaped her lips at the odd sensation. Odd and pleasurable.

"A little further," he murmured, lips on her ear. He lowered his pelvis, pushing into her slowly as she arched under him.

And then she felt the pain. She bit back a cry, clamping down on her lip with her teeth as she held her breath.

Joe stroked her cheek tenderly with his thumb, kissed her once on the mouth. And then he thrust all the way in.

This time she couldn't hold back her scream. It rang out into the air as searing agony deprived her of her senses. Her muscles and nerves all snapped tight, fighting off the dreadful invasion.

"I'm sorry," Joe whispered in her ear.

I'm sorry. Sorry you've just ruined your own life, burned up and wasted your gift, thrown away your livelihood.

Regret swelled up and twisted in her brain and her

hands tightened into fists over his back as the fiery pain blazed between her legs.

Inside her Joe rested and waited. He kissed her ear, nuzzled her cheek with his nose. Whispered, "The pain won't last forever."

Won't it?

She'd never felt anything like the excruciating, fiery, tearing sensation.

Joe kissed her cheek. "You're a real virgin." He chuckled. "Intact. That's pretty rare I think."

"Even rarer now," she hissed through tight lips. "Have you deflowered a lot of virgins?"

She instantly regretted her rude, cruel remark. *It's the pain talking.*

"Never." He paused, nuzzling her cheek again. "You're only the second woman I've slept with."

"What?"

Her eyes sprang open. Joe's face hovered just over hers, and he kissed her softly on the lips before replying.

"I married young. I never slept with anyone but my wife. My ex-wife."

"Oh."

"So it's all new to me, too." He blinked, his dark eyes unreadable in the semidarkness.

"I'm sorry," she whispered. "I would have liked it to be good for you."

"We're not done yet." He brushed her brows with his lips, kissed her eyelids as her eyes closed again.

The pain was subsiding. The smarting sting of it gave way to a throb of pleasure. A pulse of warmth. And then another.

Joe stroked her hair and kissed her neck, soothing her.

The thickness of him shifted slightly inside her,

setting off a tremor that rippled through her, relaxing her muscles.

"You okay?" His breath smelled of cinnamon, trailing over her mouth.

She nodded, eyes still closed, limbs heavy. He kissed her lips and they parted. Their tongues tangled together and heat bloomed in her mouth. Greedily she kissed him, and her arms twined around him, holding him tight.

The hunger crept through her body like a brush fire, sending her fingers roving over his back, lifting her pelvis to bury him deeper inside her. His hips returned the pressure, rising and falling with hers in a controlled tango. She writhed, enjoying the sensation of his thickness filling her, of his big warm, healthy body in her arms. Enjoying the subtle play of his lips, the throb of his intense arousal.

Who are you, Joe Figueroa?

The man surrounding her with his powerful embrace, covering her face with rough kisses, was an intriguing blend of bravado and vulnerability, anger and tenderness.

He thrust into her, triggering a blast of pure pleasure that shivered through her limbs. Her moan filled the room as her head tipped back in abandon.

Joe traced a line of soft kisses along her jaw and over the sensitive skin of her neck. His rhythmic movements rocked her further and further into a strange realm of unfamiliar and blissful sensation. His hands swept over her skin, stirring every part of her into an inferno of arousal that threatened to erupt and implode.

As the first wave of uncontrollable climactic madness surged through her and threatened to break its bounds, she tried to fight back. She squeezed her eyes shut and clenched her fists, afraid to lose control.

Joe stroked her hair and caressed her cheek, never breaking the rhythm pushing her over the brink of sanity.

"Let go," he whispered, his hot breath shimmering over her damp skin. "Let it all go."

And she did. She forgot about her powers, her family, her legacy. She forgot about her job, her apartment, her new dress. She forgot about the world, the past, the future, even the present. She let go of each thought, one by one, until there was nothing left but her and Joe, moving together in a storm of uncontrollable sensation and unleashed emotion.

The explosion began at her center, right where Joe filled her, and unfurled like a cyclone, widening and thickening, spreading through her limbs in a wave of contractions and spasms that sparkled along her muscles and nerves.

She heard her cries as if they were coming from far away. She heard Joe's answering shout as his own climax blasted through both of them. The boundaries between them disappeared as they became one shuddering, hot, damp, heaving tangle of limbs and mouths and hearts.

Joe collapsed heavily on top of her, clinging to her, breathless. She whimpered, unable to summon even the tiniest shred of sensible thought. Instead, she clung to him like driftwood after a shipwreck, until sanity and consciousness began to return in stray wisps.

"Am I crushing you?" he rasped huskily.

"Yes," she squeaked. "But I like it."

His throaty chuckle rocked through both of them, and he lifted himself slightly, easing the pressure on her torso. He rolled onto his side, still holding her tightly, her breasts crushed pleasantly against his chest.

"That was amazing," she whispered into his shoulder, suddenly shy.

"You were amazing," he whispered into her ear. "How do you feel?"

"Good." She paused, letting her lashes flicker against his skin. "Free."

She pulled her head back and looked him straight in the eyes. A smile flickered across his face.

"Free is a good thing to be." He raised his thumb and pushed back a stray strand of her now-wild hair.

"And what about you?"

"What about me?" he glanced at his hand as it played in her hair.

"How do you feel?" She said it softly, cautiously.

"Very, very satisfied." He looked at her and raised his eyebrows. He tried to push a smile to his lips, but it faltered and he hid it in a kiss on her cheek. Her heart shrank a little as he brushed off her loaded question. What had she hoped for? That he'd feel renewed, rebuilt, healed?

She still really didn't know anything about him. And his baggage wasn't her business. For once in her life she'd acted on impulse, done what *she* wanted. And she'd wanted Joe. Wanted to hold him, to kiss him, to do all that other hot, messy, crazy stuff adults do when they like each other.

He rested his head on his hand, propped up on one elbow, his other hand rearranging the stray locks of hair that fell over her face and shoulders. His lids were lowered, his focus on her hair, avoiding her glance. She'd wanted to have sex with him, to give into all those primal urges he'd sparked up in her. And she'd promised herself that she wouldn't want more.

But something inside her started to ache a little as he

excused himself and went to the bathroom to clean up. And the ache only subsided when he returned and settled himself back on the bed with her. Instinctively she scooted toward him over the warm sheets and snuggled up against him.

A muscle twitched in his cheek, and she lifted her hand to stroke it. As she touched his skin, a little shiver of tenderness sprang along her arm and echoed in her belly.

Had she used him? Hurt him somehow?

He'd wanted her for his own reasons. Pretty simple ones, too. The usual reasons a man wants a woman.

His hand slid along her hair to rest on her waist, then drifted over her backside, soft and sensual. He was attracted to her as a woman. And that made her feel good. Powerful, even.

It was enough to be wrapped in strong arms and held tightly. To feel, just for a while, that she wasn't so alone.

She resisted an impulse to try and peer into the future, to look for glimpses of what might happen. Even to see if she still could.

Don't do it, Susana. Live in the present. Enjoy what you have for what it is and don't ask for more.

She buried her face in Joe's shoulder, and his musky male aroma soothed and settled her. His hand played over her back a little, then settled comfortably around her as they both drifted into a deliciously relaxed sleep.

Joe woke up totally enveloped in Susana. Their arms and legs intertwined, their torsos huddled together, her hair over his face and her sweet breath filling his nostrils as she inhaled and exhaled with the slow, steadiness of a deep sleep.

Oh lord, this felt way too good.

She'd woken him twice during the night, hungry for more lovemaking. Each time his body had responded instantly and totally. Now sexual satisfaction mingled enticingly with fresh arousal as he became aware of her gorgeous body entwined with his. Pure pleasure crept through him, lighting each synapse, one by one, to blissful awakening.

Light poured in through the uncurtained windows. The apartment faced west, to the river, so they were spared the full blast of the sunrise or the prying eyes of people in a neighboring building.

Susana's warm, relaxed body filled his arms. He'd never slept like this with Linda. She'd liked her space. If they'd made love in bed she'd always turned away from him, shutting him out before falling asleep. When Susana had embraced him, wanting to hold him even after the main event was over, he'd been in danger of losing it and had to batten down the hatches pretty quick.

And as he looked at Susana—her face sweetly serious as always, her black mane strewn over the pillow and over him—a surge of wild, mad happiness leaped inside him.

Uh-oh.

He'd come into this situation feeling lonely and horny, looking for a little diversion. Susana wanted to make love for her own odd reasons. They'd both come here with their eyes wide open.

No promises.

He didn't have anything to offer her. His moving parts might still be in good working order, but deep inside the machinery was broken and the cost of repair was just too high.

She was young and beautiful, unspoiled, a twenty-three-year-old virgin for crying out loud. Well, she'd been one until last night anyway. He'd taken enough from her.

So why did the thought of waking up without her threaten to squeeze the breath from his lungs?

She exhaled audibly, a sweet tiny moan, and her hot breath tickled the hairs on his face. Bliss. He opened his eyes and saw a secret smile creeping across her beautiful plum colored lips.

Was she thinking about him?

She felt wonderfully relaxed, sleeping like a baby with her body totally enclosed in his. Why did they fit together so well? Why did he feel so damn good with her?

Was there really something to that whole woman-you're-destined-to-marry thing?

Don't even go there, Joe.

He heard his phone ring in the living room. Life summoning him back on deck. Probably one of the potential clients he'd called yesterday. But he wasn't going to disentangle himself from the lovely Susana one moment before he had to.

The high-pitched bleeping must have penetrated her dreams, because he could see her eyes moving rapidly beneath her eyelids. Then her lashes flickered a little.

He almost held his breath as she opened her eyes, as if she might be surprised—horrified even—to be confronted by the sight of him first thing in the morning.

But her eyes shone, soft and sleepy. Her smile deepened before she inclined her head slightly to give him a kiss on the cheek. Sweet Jesus. His heart was doing something crazy in there, and already he was getting hard again.

His arousal pressed gently into the soft flesh of her belly, and she wiggled against it, sending tremors through him that made him swallow hard.

"Morning," she whispered.

"Hi Susana," he rasped.

She glanced away for a second, lowering the curtain of her thick lashes. Then she looked up at him, night-colored eyes shimmering. "Thank you for making last night...beautiful."

Uh-oh. Joe shoved down a crazy riot of emotion churning in his chest. Threatening to make him do something embarrassing, like start singing hallelujahs or bawling like a baby.

"It was my pleasure." His voice came out a little husky but okay.

"I enjoyed sleeping with you, too."

"The feeling is mutual." Phew. If he could just keep spurting out platitudes maybe he'd get through this without making an ass of himself.

"You're really comfy..." she blinked. "For someone so hard."

Laughter bubbled up in him, releasing the tension. "Firm mattresses are good for the posture. Not that yours needs any help."

His hand still rested on her back and he stroked the skin—delicious warm velvet—on his way to giving her backside a playful squeeze.

She wiggled again and snuggled tighter against him.

Oh, Susana.

Between his cock stiffening and his heart hammering he was ready to burst into flames any second. "You're something else, woman."

She giggled. "I feel like a woman this morning. I wondered if I'd feel different, and I do."

"How?"

"I don't know how to explain it." She pursed her lips thoughtfully. "I feel bolder somehow, like I've grown up. I'm ready to take on the world."

"Sounds dangerous." He winked.

"I'm turning my whole life around. I'm going to do what I want from now on." She lifted her chin, as if defying him to argue.

"Oh yeah?"

"I'm going to take the GED exam. I'm going to apply to school. And in the meantime I'm going to find a real job that comes with an actual paycheck, not a bunch of sweaty five-dollar bills pressed into my hand." She paused, bit her lip, then spoke. "I've been a prisoner of tradition all my life. Now I'm going to find my own way."

At that moment a shadow passed across her face. Not a metaphorical one but a real one, as a bird—a seagull or a pigeon maybe?—swooped close to the window. She glanced up quickly and frowned.

"What is it?" he asked, when she remained unmoving, staring out the window, almost a full minute later. "Is that some kind of sign?"

"I don't know. Maybe." She looked worried.

"I thought you weren't going to pay attention to that stuff any more."

"I guess old habits die hard." She spoke slowly, still looking past Joe and out the window. Then she shook her head and forced a smile to her lips. "Ugh, I really do need to stop letting all that traditional stuff mess with my head. Like I said, I'm starting a new life, and from now on..."

A loud banging sound interrupted her words.

"What the hell?" Joe flinched out of their embrace,

adrenaline firing his blood.

The banging thundered through the apartment.

Joe leaped off the bed. The door to the living room was open, and he quickly identified the sound as being a fist pounding hard on the metal front door to his apartment.

"Susana!" yelled a voice from the other side of the huge door. Then a different voice, also male, "Open up, before I smash it down."

"Oh, no," whispered Susana. "It's my cousins."

9

Susana's face blanched with panic, and she clutched the sheet about herself. "Don't open it!"

"How would they know you're here?"

She shook her head, eyes wide with terror. "I don't know, maybe they went to my apartment and found the note you left with your address."

Joe took a few steps into the living room, grabbed his jeans off the floor and tugged them on.

"No, Joe, don't open it," she pleaded, her voice reedy. "They'll kill you."

"No one's going to kill anyone."

"You don't know them, Joe... Please, I'm begging you."

He picked up her dress and tossed it to her. "Put this on."

Maybe he said it too harshly, because her lip quivered and tears welled in her eyes. She remained frozen on the bed, kneeling with the sheet clutched around her. The hammering and shouting became louder and more insistent.

"I'll take care of them," he said softly. He walked to her and stroked her cheek, wiping away a tear with his thumb. "I won't let them hurt you."

He turned and walked toward the door.

"Don't!" She shouted loud enough for the men on the other side of the door to hear.

"I knew it! Susana! She's in there!" Boots kicked at the metal, and Joe heard something being thrust into the lock.

Anger fired his gut as he strode to the door. He'd be damned if he'd let anyone threaten Susana, and he certainly wasn't going to cower behind a locked door in his own apartment.

"Don't force the lock. I'm opening it."

The silence from the other side of the door was more eerily threatening than the shouting and banging of a few seconds earlier.

Joe pulled back the ancient deadbolt. He hoped Susana had her dress on by now. He sucked in a breath as he tugged the lever that opened the door and slid it aside.

Two men stood on the other side, glaring at him with black eyes very much like Susana's.

"She's here," hissed one. "I heard her."

"Yes," Joe said coolly. "She's here."

Both men were tall, black haired, with intense faces. One looked a little older than the other, maybe mid-thirties. Joe quickly took in the details and assessed the situation.

No unconcealed weapons, except teeth-baring rage.

The younger one tried to push past him, but Joe caught his arm and held him back. The older one stared at Joe, narrowing his eyes and fixing him with a stare that bored through his skin like a laser.

"You can come in only if you promise not to hurt Susana."

"Hurt Susana? I'd slit my own throat first, you *gadjo*

scum." The man in Joe's grasp raised his fist but stopped an inch from making contact with his chin. He pulled his fist back. "We'd never hurt her. We look out for her."

Joe glanced from him to the older cousin, who still regarded him with his chilling stare.

"Can you respect my home?"

They both just looked at him.

"Well, can you?"

The grunts they gave could be taken as assent or not. He decided to give them the benefit of the doubt.

"Then, come in." He stood aside and ushered them into the room, then closed the door.

The open door to the bedroom revealed Susana, hastily clad in her rumpled burgundy dress, her hair wild, falling about her shoulders.

Damn, he'd never seen a more intoxicating sight. He almost forgot about the two menacing goons beside him as blood rushed from his brain to his groin.

"What has this *gadjo* done to you?"

Susana obviously wasn't there on a palm-reading housecall. Her red and swollen lips, her glowing skin and wild hair all painted her as a woman who has made mad, passionate love in the very recent past. The twin spots of color high on her cheeks darkened under her cousin's gaze.

"I'm here of my own free will," she said, her voice a little unsteady. "Joe is my friend."

"You've had sex with him, haven't you?" said the older one, his voice low and controlled.

"Yes." She lifted her chin, and Joe saw her swallow.

The younger man clenched his fists. The older turned to Joe and looked hard at him, shaking his head. "You don't know what you've done." He stared into his eyes, and Joe stared back, unblinking. The piercing black gaze wandered down over Joe's torso, his lip curling as he took in the tattoo and scar before returning to his face. "You've ruined my cousin's life. You've contaminated her. From now on, she will always be unclean."

Joe heard Susana whimper, and he froze, not wanting to take his eyes off the man. Not sure how to respond. What did he know about the gypsy world? Maybe he had ruined her life.

"No Romani man will want her now. She'll be an outcast, a pariah." He looked past Joe to Susana. "Do you still have the third eye?"

"I don't know. I don't care." Susana's determined tone made Joe turn to her. "I'm tired of being a professional gypsy all the time. I don't have to make a living telling fortunes. I'm intelligent, I'm hard working, and I want a real life."

"Susana." The older man shook his head, his face grim. "You know the *gadjo* world is not your home. You know what happened to your mother." He fixed her with his fierce stare. "She tried to live among the *gadje*, and it killed her."

"Did it kill her? Or did the family kill her to end the embarrassment of her living with a *gadjo* man?"

Both men froze, staring at her. "This *gadjo* scum is planting his filthy ideas in your mind. Our family is not a gang of murderers." The younger man had finally spoken, and he still held his fists clenched, ready for use.

"Don't treat me like a child. I know what our family is and isn't."

"Do not speak of the family in front of a *gadjo*." The older man said it quietly.

Susana glanced at Joe. Suspiciously. Suddenly he really did feel like a *gadjo*, whatever that was. "Listen," he said, "I'm not interested in airing anyone's family laundry. Susana's a grown woman who can make her own choices. She doesn't need to be chaperoned or bossed around by you."

"You don't understand," said the younger man. "She is a Romani woman. Our ways are different."

"She's only half gypsy," Joe interrupted.

"Even one drop makes her all gypsy," intoned the older man quietly. "We take care of our own."

"Susana can take care of herself."

The younger man snorted. "See! This scum is not even offering to take care of you, Susana. He's used you up and now he'll throw you aside. He has another woman's name tattooed on his arm."

"That's my mom's name. Maria. I had it inked there when she died."

"Yeah, right," said the younger man. The older man raised an eyebrow.

"What do I care if you believe me? Susana knows I won't lie to her."

There was a long, awkward silence.

He had once had another woman's name tattooed on his arm. He'd pledged his life to her and given her almost a decade of it. Burning her name off his arm had left it scarred, along with his heart. He knew he was damaged goods.

He hadn't promised Susana anything beyond one night. Maybe they thought he really had screwed up her life and was about to leave her twisting in the wind?

Maybe they were right.

The thought twisted in his gut like a knife.

"Susana," the older one crossed his arms over his

chest and looked at her. "Do you wish to marry this man?"

Susana looked panicked, her face suddenly white, lips quivering. "I...I... No."

Joe's heart palpitated out of control as she hesitated, but at the sound of Susana's, *no,* it deflated like a balloon. He swallowed hard and drew back his shoulders.

"Because if you wish to marry him..." He paused and glanced at Joe with disdain. "He *will* marry you."

"No. No." Susana's voice quavered, and tears filled her eyes.

Why did it hurt so damn much to hear her say no?

"See, *gadjo* scum, she doesn't even want you."

Something surged inside Joe as the younger man sneered at him. Next thing he knew he'd grabbed the front of the kid's leather jacket and flung him to the floor, sprawling on top of him. His knees hit the wood hard and the jacket zipper scraped his knuckles.

"Joe!" Susana's panicked voice squeezed his heart.

The tide of rage ebbed, leaving regret in its wake. "Look, I'm sorry." He loosened his hold on the kid and scrambled to his feet. "I don't want to start anything ugly. Could you just lay off calling me *gadjo* scum? It's getting on my nerves."

"We're all adults here," said Susana. "Step away from each other, and we'll start this over. I'll introduce you, and you can meet each other like normal people. Okay?"

Joe nodded.

"Joe, this is my cousin Janus." Janus, back on his feet, scowled at him and brushed imaginary dust from his jacket. "And this is my cousin Roman," she indicated the older man in the incense-reeking coat, who hadn't moved a muscle. "They've looked out for me since I was born. I love them like brothers, even though they don't know when to stop treating me like a baby."

She pushed her hair back with her hand. "Janus and Roman, this is Joe Figueroa. He's a good man."

"How do you know?" asked Janus.

"Because I know."

Joe knew she was fibbing. She didn't know him well enough to say with any assurance that he was good. He wouldn't even make that claim himself, but he was grateful all the same.

He looked from one to the other. "As Susana said, she came here of her own free will. She's an adult, she can make her own choices."

Susana moved until she stood next to him, presenting a united front against the two intruders. He half expected her to take his hand, and the flesh of his palm began to heat in anticipation. But she tossed her hair again, lifted her chin and crossed her hands over her chest.

"As Joe said, from now on I'll be making my own choices. I've been a prisoner of this family too long. I've lived like a nun and worked like a slave since I was thirteen. I would have done anything for Granna, but she's gone now, and it's time for a change."

"Susana." Roman spoke slowly. "You don't know what you're doing."

"I know what I'm doing, all right. I'm taking charge of my own life, and if anyone doesn't like it, they can keep their thoughts to themselves."

Joe shot a glance at her and took in the confident tilt of her chin with a swell of pride. He was genuinely glad to see her stand up for herself.

"But the family..." Janus hurled his words out like

fists, and as he trailed off the unspoken ones seemed to clang together in the air around them.

"The family will only know as much as you tell them," said Susana. "I don't want to hurt anyone, but I can't live someone else's life any more."

"Susana." Roman's eyes narrowed. "You are Granna's successor. It's your duty to help shape the direction we all go in."

She blew out a frustrated snort. "I'm twenty-three years old, for crying out loud! I can barely figure out what direction I want to go in when I leave my apartment. I have no business telling a bunch of other people what to do."

"You have the power."

"The power to what? See the future? Who cares about the future? We're all living in the here and now." Her voice was getting shrill, and Joe could see her starting to tremble. "I've lived my life for everyone else until now, and I have to start living for me."

She was on the verge of tears from the sound of it. Joe stepped forward. "I think you should leave now. You can see I'm not keeping Susana here by force."

He couldn't help but notice Janus's disdainful glance at his tattooed torso, and he raised his shoulders. He was taller than both of them, fitter too. Not that it mattered, since he had no intention of indulging in any more Neanderthal antics.

"I'm staying," she said firmly.

Roman nodded, his face grim. "As you wish." His long coat swished as he turned to the door, and the resulting tang of incense tickled Joe's nose. Why on earth was he wearing a coat in midsummer? *Don't ask.* Janus followed close behind him, jaw clenched, a faithful pit bull deprived of a chance to draw blood.

As the door clanged behind them, Susana let out an audible breath of relief.

"See? No one's dead." He turned to face her fully for the first time since her cousins interrupted their lovely morning in bed. She still held her chin high, but her hands were trembling and her face chalky.

He reached out and cupped her cheek with his palm. "You took a stand, Susana. And they listened."

She nodded. He pushed back a loose strand of hair. She still looked wonderfully unkempt, wild, her dress slipping off her shoulder. He slid his hand down her soft neck to where the slim bones of her shoulder lay bared.

"You're a woman now," he whispered. She shivered slightly as he placed one hand at her waist. She softened, and on instinct his hand rose to her breast. He covered the soft roundness with his palm, feeling her nipple tighten under his flesh.

Testosterone and adrenaline still roared through his system, and apparently the feeling was mutual. Susana reached out and snatched his ear roughly, tugging him toward her. He seized her around the waist, almost knocking her off her feet. As she thrust her cool tongue into his mouth, a flame of arousal speared up inside him.

Their tongues tangled, and he grabbed at her dress, shoving it down over her lush curves, pushing it past the delicious fullness of her hips and thighs. She moaned, the sound vibrating through him, as her nails scored his back and shoulders.

"I want you, now," she rasped, breath hot on his neck. She slid down the length of his body, arms around him. Her breasts grazed his torso and brushed against his hard arousal for a moment before gliding over his shuddering thighs as she pulled down his jeans.

As he stepped out of the pants, almost falling, she

stretched herself out on the floor of his unfurnished living room.

Sunbeams danced over her body, making it shimmer golden in the morning light. Her black hair splayed over the shining floorboards.

"Oh, no."

"What?" Her eyes were black with desire, her lips flushed dark.

"No more protection. We used up all the condoms."

"No!" Susana rolled onto her side, burying her face in her hands. He squatted on the floor beside her and stroked her backside, then slipped a finger into the hot wetness of her sex. She writhed against his finger as he thrust it deeper and caressed her with his thumb. Almost immediately he felt the quivering muscles that signaled her release.

"I want to please you, too," breathed Susana. "But I don't know how."

"Licking works well," he murmured, almost deranged at the sight of her face glowing under the tangled mane of black hair.

She flashed a dangerous glance at him, climbed over him, then stuck out her dark berry tongue and licked his lips with it. The resulting shiver shook him from head to toe. She trailed her tongue over his torso, following the hollow between his pectorals down to his belly button. His skin jumped in response.

His erection quivered as she drew near, anticipating the caress of her hot mouth. As she lowered her lips over his painfully aroused flesh, his eyes closed and he gave himself over to the agonizingly intense sensation as she licked and sucked him to the point of total madness.

His heart stretched almost to bursting as the rush of his orgasm shook his limbs, and he clutched Susana to his chest.

He didn't want her to leave. Ever. He wanted to hold her safe in his arms until the world stopped spinning and faded away. The past and future evaporated in the mist of pleasure fogging his senses and nothing was left but the sweet immediacy of their embrace.

Even on the hard wooden floor of his apartment they fit together like a hand and glove, and he wasn't sure which was which. Didn't care either. He just knew everything was a hundred percent perfect at that moment.

Susana sighed, snuggling even closer inside the circle of his arms. Their lovemaking was so raw and steamy, the aftermath so tender. He was coming completely undone and it felt way too good.

The phone rang again.

Joe groaned and hugged Susana tighter. "Don't go. Don't ever go."

There he'd said it. He really did want her to stay. Was that so crazy? She could move in with him, even bring the mean old parrot if she wanted. They'd get to know each other quick enough. *Sometimes you just have to go with your gut.*

"I have to leave. I have appointments this morning." Her voice was husky.

"Blow them off. You're giving all that up, anyway."

"Not so fast. I have to pay the rent."

"No, you don't. You could come live here." There, cards spilled all over the table.

She pulled her head back and stared at him. "I suspect some part of your body other than your brain is talking."

"That may be partly true, but we're good together. Maybe there's something to that destiny racket you've been peddling."

Susana didn't reply right away and Joe held his breath. Damn, she already meant so much to him. He'd bargained on hot sex, not on wanting so much more. How had he gotten way over his head so quickly?

"I've always believed my destiny is to cherish my gift as a seer and devote my life to my people." She squeezed her eyelids closed, as if hit by a sudden headache.

"But you don't think that any more, right?"

"No..." She pressed her face into his shoulder. "I don't know. I don't know what I believe any more. I'm trying to figure it out. Don't rush me, okay?"

"Okay." Rushing in without knowing all the facts. That's what got him into a jam ten years ago. He'd taken lust for love and paid the high price of betrayal.

Betrayal. The third card. The memory of their last reading hit him. He'd been so doped with lust at the sight of her naked body he hadn't paid too much attention to the cards. But she'd warned him. He'd sworn he'd never let a woman hurt him again, and here he was laying himself out on the floor like a rug to be trampled.

They didn't know each other. But did anyone ever truly know another person? He'd changed so much just since he'd met her. Last week he'd been an empty husk of a man incapable of feeling anything except raw anger. Now he felt alive, tender, capable of feeling way too much. And Susana had done that to him.

"You're magic," he whispered. "And I don't mean because of your powers."

She opened her eyes and flashed him a warm glance that heated his blood. "You've made me feel beautiful. I've never felt that before."

"You're the most beautiful woman in the universe."

He pushed his fingers into her thick, silky hair. "The most beautiful woman in the history of the world."

"I bet you say that to all the girls."

"Don't forget there have only been two girls, and the first was a case of mistaken identity." He narrowed his eyes, "I went to this fortune-teller, you see..." He trailed off deliberately and they both shook with silent laughter.

"I can't believe you never slept with anyone else!"

"I'm a one-woman man."

"You're something else, Joe." She pushed their torsos apart slightly and traced his long scar with her finger. "That wound must have been bad enough to kill you."

His skin shivered where she grazed her nail over the raised line of flesh. "So they tell me. There've been times I wish it did."

He should tell her what happened. Let her know who he really was. Would she still want to be with him?

The phone rang again.

"Someone wants to get hold of you pretty badly." She raised a slim black brow.

"Maybe it's for you? Your family didn't seem to have any trouble finding you here."

"I've got to get my locks changed. Now Granna's gone I don't need the whole gang trouping in and out when they're in the neighborhood."

The shrill beeping rang through the still air of the apartment. Joe groaned and rolled back, his skin aching at the loss of contact with Susana's warm satin flesh.

He scrambled to his feet and grabbed the phone. As he made an appointment to meet with the CIO of Drake Morgan Investments that afternoon, he watched Susana dress herself and attempt to tug his comb through her hair.

He hung up the phone. "We haven't had breakfast yet."

"I have to go."

"Call me. Or just come see me."

She nodded, and pushed a lock of hair awkwardly behind her ear. He reluctantly tugged on his jeans. He didn't want to open the door.

Her goodbye kiss stung his lips, pleasure torquing with pain at the thought of parting from her, even for a minute.

Don't go! He kept the words to himself, knowing they wouldn't keep her. She'd been prisoner to other people's needs for too long. She needed to taste her freedom and find her own way to what she wanted.

She didn't say goodbye, just turned from him and walked down the short hallway to the stairs. When he heard the metal door downstairs close with a loud clang, he knew with chilling certainty that she wouldn't come back.

10

Susana was in the back room counting the day's earnings when she heard someone enter the shop. The bell over the door tinkled, and she groaned. She'd wrapped up all her appointments and wanted to get home to a hot bath. Or a cool bath. Anything to try and soothe the ache racking her muscles, to quell the prickle of her skin, to ease the uncomfortable thudding of her heart that assaulted her whenever she thought of Joe.

Joe.

He occupied her thoughts from dawn to dusk and all the hours in between. He haunted her in dreams, the scent of him, the feel of his arms around her, mocked her as she lay alone in bed, tossing and turning in the summer heat.

There was no doubt that her powers as a seer were diminished. She'd given them up willingly, like so many women before her, choosing a life in the present over peering into the mists of the future. Choosing to know the transient yet intoxicating pleasures of the flesh. She understood now why her mother had gone astray. Had created her.

It had been four agonizing days since she'd seen him. So many times she'd been tempted to pick up the phone and call. Or her feet began to lead her restlessly westward, in the direction of his apartment.

And then each time she remembered all the reasons why they shouldn't be together. It would break the family apart. Joe and her brothers would hate each other. She'd lose the people who cared about her, and if it didn't work out with Joe—a distinct possibility— she'd be truly alone in the world.

The third card was a card of warning.

The hollow empty spaces inside her seemed to swell as she counted on her fingers all the many reasons why fooling around with Joe was stupid, senseless and could lead to nothing but heartbreak and disaster for both of them.

She heard the scrape of the chair on the old wood floor as the visitor outside in the storefront sat at the table. Ugh. She didn't have the energy to hear any more troubles today. She had enough of her own. Maybe if she just sat back here, kept silent, they'd go away. She missed the little cat that used to brush around her ankles. It had run away two years ago, and for a while she'd envied it. But for all she knew it was probably dead. Curiosity killed the...

The door to the back room flung open.

Joe.

Her skin stung as she rasped in a breath. She dropped the money she was holding and wrinkled notes fluttered to the floor.

His eyes fixed on her, shining black in the dim light. The door closed behind him, sealing them together in the dusty, cluttered storeroom behind the *ofisa*. Neither of them spoke.

He radiated energy, which rippled toward her, raising the tiny hairs on her skin, jingling her nerves.

White-hot intensity that swirled amid the dust and incense. Not anger, as she might have expected, but something far more complicated, mixed up and messy like this whole crazy affair.

Passion.

The dim light from the single bulb shone across his harsh, masculine features, highlighting his scar and the thin shadow of stubble that dusted his jaw. She could hear him breathing—or was it her own arrhythmic inhalations and exhalations that disturbed the eerie silence?

Passion could be a dangerous force when unleashed into the world. It wasn't tied to love. It could just as well be driven by hate. It conquered hearts and minds, knew no limits but its own.

Susana swallowed. She sat on a high tabletop, the only unbroken piece of furniture, and it raised her almost to eye level with Joe. She held his gaze, even as it almost cost her the ability to breathe.

"You didn't come to me." His low voice shimmered through the thick air.

"I couldn't."

"So I came to you." He didn't move.

He wore a suit, gray, with a white shirt and a dark tie loosened at the neck. The uniform of respectability. But she could see his feelings for her were anything but respectable.

The heat smoking from his gaze steamed up her body until pricks of perspiration trickled down her spine.

His eyes drifted over her face, grazing her lips and cheeks, where she felt the two familiar spots of color spring to life.

"I need you, Susana."

She could feel his need lapping toward her, splashing up against the depthless lake of her own. Every part of her ached for him.

But it wasn't simple sexual yearning any more. Something deeper. She cared about him. She wanted him to be happy.

He took a step forward, and she heard herself gasp. Her fingers flew to the edge of the table and gripped it like the edge of a precipice.

"Don't worry, I won't touch you."

Please touch me! her body cried, as fear and desire crackled through her like wildfire.

"I know you only wanted one night of pleasure," he continued, eyes narrowed. "That's all I wanted, too. We made no promises to each other." He swallowed and his Adam's apple moved above the starched white collar of his shirt. "But something happened between us. Something...magic."

The oddly incongruous word slid off his tongue and hung in the air between them.

Magic. It was magic all right. But there was good magic and bad magic. What they made was black magic—dark, intense, a dangerous force that crept out at night and drove strangers into each other's arms. The kind of enchantment that made you give up everything you'd ever known and all the people you held dear.

That wasn't the Romani way. Arranged marriage for the good of the families. Family first. Girls were married off very young, before they had a chance to make their own mistakes. She'd escaped that fate, but it didn't mean she had to go tearing off in the other direction.

Did it?

Joe took another step toward her.

"You said you'd never lie to me. Is that still true?"

She nodded dumbly.

"Can you honestly tell me you feel nothing for me?"

She shook her head. She felt far too much. Feelings she didn't understand and couldn't name.

Fire flashed in Joe's eyes, and she heard her breathing quicken. She struggled to shove down the chaotic mix of emotions swelling inside her.

Are you going to betray me, Susana?

I don't know.

Remembered wisps of conversation danced in her head as she gripped the table, willing her body not to respond to his nearness.

It was time for betrayal. To save his life. To save her own.

"Do you think I still owe you?" she said coolly, her heart seizing as she forced out the cruel words. The flicker of confusion that crossed Joe's face cut her.

"No," he spoke low. "You don't owe me anything." His features tightened. "I've taken my payment. In full."

His eyes dropped crudely to her chest, as they had when he'd first entered her *ofisa*. Her breasts stirred beneath the dark blouse, craving his touch. She felt a flush of heat rising up over her face.

"You don't owe me anything at all," he whispered. He lifted his hand almost to her breast. Her skin quivered, expecting his touch, but he just held it there.

"See, I won't touch you. No matter how much I want to." He withdrew his hand, and Susana felt it like a slap.

Touch me, her body called.

What kind of magic made a grown woman want a man's hand on her breast?

Nothing good can come of it.

"It hurt me, you know, when you told your cousins you didn't want to marry me." Joe let out a bitter laugh. "Can you imagine? At that moment I hoped you'd say yes. You feed a stray dog once, and then you can't get rid of him."

He'd come to her like a stray dog, looking for scraps of salvation. She'd fed him, too.

He cocked his head slightly. "I guess the only way to get rid of a stray is boot him out into the street. Let him know he's not wanted. Are you going to kick me out Susana?"

Yes.

The word formed in her brain, but her lips wouldn't speak it. They formed a mute O as she stared at Joe. *He wanted to marry her?* Well, he hadn't said exactly that.

When Roman had asked if she wanted to marry Joe, she'd said no to let Joe off the hook. Reassure him she expected nothing. But in fact he'd wanted her to say yes?

The idea of marrying Joe suddenly took root in her brain and blossomed into a strange and beautiful flower. Man and wife, living together, helping each other, loving and making love...

Are you nuts, Susana?

Like a daylily at dusk the flower shriveled. He didn't want to marry her. He wanted her to want to marry him. A right of first refusal. Men just want to know they have the power. That's what Granna always said.

Marriage is slavery, she'd said that too. She'd worked like a slave to support her idle husband and in turn he'd bossed and bullied her because it was his right. She'd shed only crocodile tears on his grave and was glad to get her freedom and her psychic powers back. *Don't marry, don't ever marry.* Those were Granna's only words of advice on the subject. No doubt why her own daughter had no marriage arranged and ended up living in sin with a *gadjo* and bearing his nameless bastard—her.

Tears pricked her eyelids. She'd tried hard to live a life apart, but her mother couldn't do it and now she was failing, too. A lifetime of warnings weren't enough to quiet the angry desires of the flesh.

"Go on then." Joe lifted his chin. "You have to be cruel to get rid of a stray. We don't give up easy." He stared at her, daring her to throw him out. The twinkle of amusement in his eye told her he didn't think she would. Didn't think she could.

Oh yeah?

She jumped off the table onto the floor and shoved him with her hand. He caught her wrist and held it tight, never taking his eyes off hers. Her breath caught in her throat as his grip tightened over the pulse point on her wrist.

"You're hurting me." She tried to pull her wrist away, but her thin arms were no match for his strength.

"You're hurting *me*." The muted growl of his voice stirred something down below the folds of her skirt. Something hot and dangerous. Something ugly and beautiful at the same time. Again she tried to tug her wrist back.

"Not so easy, huh? Your wrist feels the way my heart does. Someone's got it in a vise grip."

Her own heart squeezed at his words and she quickly shoved down the rising surge of emotion threatening to choke her. *Don't feel bad. You warned him.* "I told you the meaning of the third card. I told you I'd let you down."

"You've done that already, by not coming to me. But that's in the past. Where do we go from here?"

Nowhere. Everywhere. Possibilities jumped in Susana's mind, exploding like firecrackers as they bumped up against the cool core of her reason.

He softened his grip on her wrist but didn't let go. His broad thumb chafed her pulse point as he turned her wrist over and lifted her upturned palm to his face. She didn't resist.

He lowered his eyes as he pressed his lips into the soft flesh. She gasped at the warmth of his mouth, the slick wetness of his tongue in the tender hollow of her cupped palm.

Joe dropped to his knees on the floor, his lips still pressed to her palm.

"Your good suit—the floor is filthy!" The last traces of commonsense pushed the words to her lips.

"Never you mind my suit," he muttered, as he lifted the hem of her skirt with the concentration of an archeologist discovering a lost civilization.

He let the skirt fall over his shoulders as his head slipped between her legs. She couldn't see him but, oh, could she feel him. She shuddered involuntarily as his lips and tongue began a slow ascent up her thighs, lapping at her skin, teasing and tickling first one thigh, then the other. She moaned, leaning back against the table and gripping its edge to keep herself upright.

His hands slid over her feet, tracing the openings of her sensible shoes, then skimming up the inside of her calves, lighting fires under the skin. He shifted, burying his head deeper between her thighs, until the pressure of his face parted them slightly. She heard his low groan as her knees buckled and his mouth made contact with her sex.

She was aware of damp heat spreading, but she couldn't tell if it came from within her or from the pressure of his wet tongue on her panties. He licked and nibbled at her through the thin fabric, stirring her flesh until it pulsed with arousal.

She heard herself panting, a soft animal sound that scared her a little. She wanted to touch Joe, to hold him, but he was still hidden beneath her skirt. She reached behind her back and unfastened the hook at the waist, then pushed it down. As the top of his head emerged her fingers dove into his thick hair, clutching at it as he continued to suck her to new heights of fearsome pleasure.

"I think I love you, Joe." The words slipped right out. They'd sprung to her mind, and she'd said them because she had to. Because she didn't feel like holding anything back right now. All of her was soft, fluid, open and giving, as Joe sucked and kneaded the last of her inhibitions away.

He didn't stop the relentless lapping and licking, just gripped her a little tighter with his strong fingers, holding her steady as her muscles spasmed and her body shook with the force of her climax.

"I think I love you, too, Susana," he murmured, deep in the folds of her skirt, his face still buried between her thighs. "I don't know what it means but I think it all the same."

When she finally dared to open her eyes he was standing in front of her. His eyes gleamed and his lips were moist with passion and sex. She reached up and pushed back the hair she'd disarranged with her wild groping and stroked his cheek.

I think I love you.

She unbuttoned his pants and pushed them down, feeling beneath his shirttails for the thickness of his arousal.

"I lust for you," she said, smiling, then bit her lip as her fingers tingled with excitement at touching him. She wanted to laugh but no sound came out.

"Lust and love." Joe leaned forward and kissed her neck, his tongue flicking over her jugular. "Maybe we've got them confused. Who knows where one ends and the other begins?"

"Who cares," she murmured as she shoved her hips forward to rub against him, succumbing to the force of whatever crazy uncontrolled thing it was that drew them together and aroused them both to the point of madness.

He silenced her with a kiss so deep it stole her breath. Then he tugged down her panties and lifted her up onto the table before she had a chance to protest.

He sheathed himself with a condom from his pocket and entered her slowly, pushing in as she opened to receive him, each deepening of the penetration driving her to new heights of agonizing bliss. No pain, just pleasure that flooded her body and banished all doubt and fear.

They moved together, Joe thrusting as his hands clutched her backside and pulled her into a primal rhythm that echoed through her. He kissed her face all over as he filled her, then groaned in her ear, fingers digging into her as he started to lose control. His own abandon drove her over the edge again, a second climax sweeping through her as she clutched him, not sure whether she was trying to support him or save herself.

When she finally opened her eyes everything was blurry and she could feel tears on her cheeks. She was still seated on the table, and Joe leaned over her, panting, his arms wrapped around her shoulders.

"This is crazy," she murmured, lifting a hand to wipe

the tears away. Tears? She never cried in front of anyone in her life. Granna would have smacked her for showing such weakness.

"Crazy in a good way," he whispered. "I've been crazy in a bad way, and this feels different."

"I don't know, Joe, crazy is crazy." She bit her lip again, hard, trying to invoke some sensation other than the waves of pleasure washing through her from head to toe.

He wiped a hot tear away with his big thumb. "You think too much, Susana. Sometimes you've just got to feel."

So this is how it happens. She'd seen them trooping in and out of the *ofisa*. Men and women, young and old, broken-hearted and miserable because "love" didn't go the way they hoped. And she could count Joe among their number. Did "love" ever turn out right? If it did, then those people didn't come into the shop.

Love seemed like a pretty raw deal to Susana. At least with arranged marriage there was a business deal to be upheld and a bunch of brawny male relatives to make sure everyone kept their end of the bargain. Sometimes the married pair was happy, sometimes not, but this "love" business seemed to leave everyone dripping tears on the storefront's faded baize tablecloth.

And now she was getting all tangled up in it herself.

"Even if we do love each other, whatever that means." She paused. "There's no guarantee it isn't a flash in the pan."

"Life doesn't come with a money-back guarantee. You've got to take chances."

"I'm no risk taker, Joe."

"So how come you're sitting on that table with no skirt on?" He grinned.

She smacked his face lightly. "Be serious."

"Yeah? If you're so serious why are you smiling?"

"Shut up, you." She covered his mouth with her hand, but she could feel his grin broadening under it, along with her own.

He pulled her hand away from his mouth. "We're good together. We make each other feel good, and I don't mean just the sex. I like being with you. I swear to God I'm a different man since I've met you. A couple of weeks ago I wouldn't have cared if a bus hit me, but now I'm all fired up about the future because it has you in it. Simple and stupid but there it is."

She stroked his cheek. "You're a good man, Joe."

"Like you told your cousins."

"Yes."

"I think they liked me." He winked now. "I think I'd grow on them, anyway. We'd be one big happy family."

If only that were true. The claws of apprehension sprang out again and dug themselves in around her throat.

"It's not that simple."

"Nothing ever is." He shrugged.

"The family..." She paused, not sure where to start.

"The way you say that sounds like they're some big Mafia clan."

"It's not like that exactly..."

"Exactly?" Joe raised an eyebrow.

She frowned, wondering how she could make him understand. Joe tugged his pants up and fastened them. Then he crossed his arms over his chest and cocked his head, waiting.

Susana stroked her naked thighs. "It's hard to explain. My people, the Rom," she glanced up at him. "We value family above everything."

"That's good."

"Yes." She looked down. "Sometimes it's good. It's kept us together through centuries of persecution; it's kept our culture alive. But it comes at a price." She looked up again and met his eyes. "And the price is sticking to our own."

"Keeping clear of the *gadjo*." He raised his eyebrows.

"*Gadje* is the plural, but yes." She almost smiled, even though it wasn't funny. "That's how we've kept our identity."

"Cultural identity doesn't have to define your life. This is America in the twenty-first century. I'm Cuban and Italian and proud of both. You don't have to give up your Rom culture to marry someone else."

"But I would. Being Rom is an all or nothing proposition."

"Why?"

"Tradition."

"Maybe it's time for traditions to change a little."

"Tradition and change are two words that don't really go together. Janus and Roman might agree with you. They're not as old-fashioned as they'd have you believe, but the elders in my family?–no way. In Rom culture we have an expression: *marime*. It's hard to explain to a..."

"*Gadjo*."

"Yes." Now she did smile, then it withered on her lips. "*Marime* means... unclean, contaminated. If it became known that I was with you, or if we lived together, then I'd become *marime* and no Rom would be able to associate with me." She looked hard at him, her face composed. "And I mean that literally, they wouldn't be able to look at me or talk to me or even acknowledge my presence."

"Jesus."

She shrugged. "So there it is. All or nothing."

"I don't think I'd want to be part of a culture like that."

"You can't be. You're not invited." She lifted an eyebrow.

"No kidding. But why do you want to be part of it?"

She swallowed. "Again, it's hard to explain. It's something I feel..." She put her hand over her heart. "Here. Deep inside me. It's who I am. I'm proud of my people and of our journey."

Joe nodded. She could see from his face that he understood the full implication of what she said. The light had dimmed in his eyes.

"I hear what you're saying." He swallowed. "To come with me you'd have to give up..."

"Who I am."

He grimaced.

She felt her heart shrinking and shriveling inside her. A miserable organ not worthy of the man who'd touched it.

Would "her people" keep her warm at night over the next few decades? Nope. But sleeping alone was a *gadjo* tradition she'd gotten used to, and she could carry on that way if she had to.

"I won't ask you to give it all up for me. I know only too well that love can turn out to be an illusion. A delusion." He glanced away and picked up a broken part of something—an old lamp maybe? "Nothing lasts forever."

She could see he wanted to say more but held back. Maybe he'd have liked to ask her to think about it or say that if she ever changed her mind...

"I shouldn't have come." He dropped the object and stared at her. "You were trying to let me down easy, and I stormed in here and started something I had no business doing." His eyes dropped to her bare thighs, and his hand followed, stroking her skin. Sorrow pinched her heart at the tenderness of his touch. "I'm sorry, Susana."

She felt a sob rising inside her, or a howl or a shout or something else desperate and embarrassing. She jumped off the table and groped on the floor for her skirt, tugging it on and fussing around looking for her underwear as a distraction.

"I won't come to you again, so you don't have to worry about me messing up your life."

Cold shards of realization pierced her at his words. The thought of a lifetime without Joe resonated in her skull. What a long lifetime it would be.

She straightened up, brushing dust off her skirt, groping for words. "I won't ever forget you. You've changed me."

"I made you a woman." He tried to force a smile, but it died on his lips. "No. You were a woman already. A strong and proud one. I'm grateful for the time we shared."

"Me too." More hot tears accompanied her harsh whisper.

"Some things just aren't meant to be." He took a deep breath, his face tight. She could tell he still fought words that wanted to come to his lips.

Did he want to beg her to come with him? To give up everything and follow him wherever he went? Would she?

No. They both knew it.

"Goodbye, Susana."

"Goodbye, Joe." Her rasped words were barely audible. She couldn't even see him through the blur of tears that thickened and hung in her lashes.

He didn't touch her again before he turned and left. She heard the door to the storefront close softly, then the bell as he opened the front door of the *ofisa* and exited out onto the street. For good.

11

"Get a job Susana, are you nuts?" Her aunt Leticia crossed her plump arms over her ample bosom. Her heavily made-up eyes blinked frantically beneath her mane of flame-orange hair. *Don't henna your hair once it's turned grey*, Susana thought, trying to take her mind off her predicament.

"No woman in my family will work for the *gadje*." Her husband, Anton, buttoned the jacket of his suit, getting ready to leave the house for a meeting. Their three daughters played noisily about them in the big untidy living room of the Brooklyn house.

"But, Uncle, I'll need to make more money to pay the rent on my apartment. I'll lose Granna's rent control if I put my own name on the lease. The storefront too. I've been writing checks on Granna's old account for six months—forging her signature, for crying out loud. It's not legal."

"*Gadjo* laws, pah! You're paying their rent. It's all fair and square."

Susana let out a snort of dismay. "I'm paying a hundred and twenty-five dollars a month. The market rate is well over a thousand these days, even on my place. They'd love to get me out and fix the place up for some yuppies."

"So move in with us, sweetie." Leticia moved forward and rested her hands on Susana's shoulders. Susana suppressed a shudder as the soft fingers pressed into her flesh. "We've got plenty of room, and you could help me out with the girls. You know how they'd love to have you around."

Susana sighed. Is this what the future held? To become a slave at the beck and call of her domineering aunt and her three spoiled and demanding girls. To hole up in a room in their attic, hiding her school books under the mattress and sneaking off to class on a raft of excuses. At least she wouldn't be struggling to keep a roof she couldn't afford over her head. And however horrible, it would only be temporary.

"And, sweetheart. No more talk about getting a job." A huge Cheshire cat grin spread over Aunt Leticia's round red cheeks. "Because boy, do we have a husband for you. Anton and I have been up late nights talking about how to get you nicely settled now your Granna's gone. I know she had some crazy ideas about marriage, but every woman needs a good man to look after her."

Susana's heart squeezed uncomfortably.

A good man.

No. Don't think about him.

"I don't want to marry."

"Nonsense, sweetie. Every woman needs a husband and the joy of children." She cracked a smile, and gestured to her three little angels, who were busy pulling the heads off several naked Barbie dolls.

"A very good man he is. Good family. From Cincinnati, you know. Francis Melisto. Frankie, they call him."

At least she hadn't heard of him. That was probably

a good thing. But she had a feeling he'd be pretty easy to dismiss. "How old is he?"

"Well..." Aunt Letica forced her huge fake smile again. "He's been married before, I won't deny that, but then you're not young, Susana. Most girls your age have a family already."

"How old?" She raised an eyebrow, ready to laugh.

"Under fifty."

"How reassuring. But like I said, I'm not getting married. I'm going to try and find a job, and if that doesn't work out right away, I—"

"You'll be more than welcome here. But listen to me, Susana." She leaned into Susana until garlicky breath stung her nostrils. "Marriage should be your first priority. While the old lady was alive people accepted her eccentricities—your eccentricities—but now she's gone, frankly, people are talking." She fixed Susana with a beady black stare that made her throat constrict.

Cold prickles of fear stung her fingers. Had Janus or Roman said something? No, she couldn't believe they would. *People are talking.* And why wouldn't they? A Rom woman of twenty-three, never married and living alone? It was unheard of, literally.

"Anyway, sweetie, Frankie's coming here tonight. We'll get you nicely settled, don't you worry." Her aunt patted her arm. "A good dinner, we'll have tonight. And tie your hair up, it doesn't look nice hanging all over like that."

"Got to go. Appointment." Susana blew a kiss and hurried out, before the walls of the house closed in on her and crushed her as they always threatened to when she spent too much time there. She'd be back for dinner. She was nothing if not reliable. She'd be polite to "Frankie." She'd be a good girl, heck, maybe she'd even marry one day if the right eligible Rom widower showed up...

She shuddered, unable to think any touch but Joe's on her skin.

You can't have everything, Granna had intoned with monotonous regularity. *Sometimes you have nothing. But you have your people.* And coming from Granna, who'd lost her entire family, those words rang deep in her soul.

Against all the odds, Frankie was a nice guy. Early forties, decent looking. Married once to a woman who died in a car crash. He had four teenage sons who he wanted to keep in school and out of trouble. His used computer game business sounded pretty modest, which probably meant he was honest.

When Uncle Anton left them alone together, she'd brought up her plan to study psychology as a sort of test. Not only had he not looked shocked and disgusted, but he'd actually been interested and encouraging. Uncle Anton and Aunt Letty beamed with delight as they wished him good night. Everyone could see it was a match made in...wherever those kinds of things were made. She could find absolutely nothing wrong with him.

Except that she didn't love him.

And he wasn't Joe.

Susana sat cross-legged on the table in the back room of the *ofisa*. The air still seemed to hum with the energy they'd created there, to smell of sex. Her thighs tingled as she remembered the feel of his tongue on her skin...

Stop it, Susana! She growled with frustration. She'd been so cranky lately. Every single person in the family was getting on her nerves. Grating them raw. She found herself holing up in her apartment, avoiding them. Was it for this she'd sent Joe packing? If she married Frankie she'd have to move to Cincinnati anyway. She wouldn't see even those family members she could stand the sight of.

Sure, she'd be living the life of a dutiful Rom woman, but was that enough?

On the other hand, what did she have with Joe anyway? They'd spent a little time together. Enjoyed each other's company. Her body had opened like a night-blooming orchid under his gentle touch.

Love, huh?

Sure felt like it. Especially the part that hurt like poison in her system.

Would it be so wrong to see him one more time? Just to see. *To see what? If it was real?*

The chemistry between them was so powerful that good sense—any kind of sense—flew out the window when they were together. If she went to see him they'd be tugging each other's clothes off and she wouldn't be any wiser, only in deeper.

But what if she really *was* meant to spend her life with Joe? Should she throw away her true destiny for the sake of dusty "tradition"?

Could any harm come of doing a quick reading on the seeing globe? She'd never deliberately attempted to see into her own future. But would one little peek be so wrong?

She jumped down from the table and pushed out into the front room. The globe shone, filled with promise. Such a precious thing, bought by her grandmother with money she'd scraped together cleaning houses when she first came to New York. It was over a hundred years old and wrapped in legends.

Susana touched the smooth glass and felt the buzz of energy that hummed about its reflective surface. Her powers were still there, weaker, diminished by distraction, but thrumming at the core of her consciousness. They weren't much consolation though, for the loss of Joe's warm, strong arms around her.

She sat in her chair and arranged her skirt comfortably around her legs. Apprehension tightened her stomach muscles and pricked her fingertips as she moved them toward the glass again, ready to begin.

She looked past the reflection of her own face, distorted by the curve of the orb, into the inner core where the visions appeared. For a moment she didn't see anything at all, and she prepared to turn away in relief, then an image flickered to life, like the ghosting on an old television set. She found herself looking at a man.

At Joe.

He was alone. Sitting on a bed. He wore a suit, maybe the same gray suit he'd worn when he last came to visit her. He held his head in his hands so she couldn't see his face, but she'd know him anywhere.

Cold fingers of sadness clasped around her heart. He looked so alone. She gasped as he moved, sitting up and leaning backward to stretch out on the bed.

You're not seeing the future, Susana. This is the present.

She knew it with sudden certainty. Joe sat alone in his apartment. Her feet itched to run there and see him.

Would it be so wrong?

Yes. It would be. To go visit him and then leave to marry Frankie?

The image faded. Concentrate! She didn't want to lose sight of him, even though the vision told her nothing about her own future or anyone else's.

The picture sharpened and she watched him lift his head and stare at the ceiling. Even though the image was tiny, the colors muted, she could see his eyes. Black and empty. Her belly quivered, and she felt like an intruder, stealing into his room.

Go to him. Be with him. Adrenaline sizzled in her muscles, goading her.

Don't do it, Susana! An opposing plea buzzed in her head. A thousand ancestral whispers begging her.

She rose from her chair and locked up the *ofisa*. Sunset drenched the city in syrupy golden light as she strode along the sidewalk, down Second Avenue, along Houston Street, and south to Tribeca.

To Joe's apartment.

A young couple were going into the building as she arrived so she didn't have to ring the buzzer. She avoided the elevator, needing the slower journey of the stairwell to collect herself. She climbed, each step weighed down by a growing sense of unease and an opposing jingle of mad anticipation.

By the time she reached his apartment on the fifth floor, her stomach churned and her breath came in irregular bursts, despite her efforts to be calm.

She could turn around and leave and no one would be any the wiser.

She put her finger on the doorbell and pushed. As she heard the chime sound through the apartment, her insides curled up into a knot and she gripped her arms.

No sound came from inside. Not even the scurry of a visiting mouse. Was she wrong? Maybe her "vision" was a delusion? Maybe he was out on the town with a beautiful woman? Or just busy working. Maybe it was only wishful thinking that he'd be lying on the bed, missing her.

That's what she'd thought all those years ago. *It's just wishful thinking*, the vision of you and that handsome young sailor walking arm in arm.

She pressed the doorbell, and again the chime rang through the apartment, the sound reflecting off bare walls and floor. But this time something stirred. She heard footsteps on the wood. Her ribcage tightened like steel bands around her heart and lungs, squeezing her breath out as she waited, eyes fixed on the gray paint of the door.

A surge of adrenaline shook her as she heard the bolt pulled back. As the massive door slid aside, she caught her breath and held it.

"Susana."

She'd been wrong about the clothes because he wasn't wearing a suit. Or maybe he'd just taken it off. His crumpled white shirt hung unbuttoned over faded jeans, revealing a shadowed glimpse of the eagle on his chest.

But she'd been right about the eyes. Not bright and lively as they'd been when she last saw him, they were black and lightless, hollow and empty. A muscle ticked in his cheek.

"I had to see you." Her words bounced off the hard surfaces around them, hushing her to a whisper. "I missed you." Her voice cracked, the words loaded with emotion she hadn't allowed herself to feel. She'd missed him so much it ached in her bones.

"Come in." He stepped aside to let her pass through the doorway. As she walked by him her nerves screamed at her to touch him, but she held her fists tight, pressed against her skirt. He pushed the heavy door closed, and it thudded into place.

For a moment she hoped he'd say something, give

her some direction to head in, but he didn't. He stood watching her, his expression unreadable.

She realized her arms had wrapped themselves around her waist, hugging her, perhaps giving her the comfort she wanted from Joe. "I couldn't stop thinking about you."

He didn't reply.

Had she hoped he'd run to her and say, "I love you. Will you marry me?" The squeeze in her stomach told her she had, even though she didn't know what her answer would be. For a girl who used to be able to see the future, she couldn't even handle the present too well any more.

That's what happens when you try to give up your powers. And find yourself in the grip of something far more powerful.

"I had to come." She whispered it, afraid anything louder would come out like a shout.

The muscle ticked in Joe's cheek again, and he ran a hand through his hair, tugging at it. "You shouldn't be here. If your family finds out..."

"I know." She lifted an arm and held it out, palm up. Joe hesitated for a moment before raising his own arm very slowly and extending his hand toward hers.

Her palm buzzed with the expectation of his touch, but instead she found herself enveloped in his embrace. His arms wrapped around her waist as hers flew to his neck, eagerly gripping him and holding him to her. His big hands, flat on her back, hugged her to him. As she clung to him, a swell of emotion emerged as a choking sob, muffled in the collar of his shirt.

The scent of his warm skin filled her nostrils, soothing her like precious incense. Lifting her lips she kissed the bare skin at his neck.

"Don't..." he rasped. She felt a shudder ripple through the hard muscles of his torso. He pulled back, seizing her waist in his hands and tugging her away from him. "We can't. It doesn't make sense."

"Nothing makes sense any more," she murmured, trying to keep back the tears burning her throat. His fingers dug into her waist as he held her at bay. She wanted so badly to sink back into his embrace. Her fingers had been pulled from his back as he pushed her away, and she gripped his arms, feeling the thick muscle though the stiff cotton of his shirt. Feeling his strength and wanting to rest in it.

"My uncle has found a husband for me." She couldn't look at him while she said it. He stiffened, and his fingers dug a little deeper into the flesh at her waist.

He was silent for a moment, then his voice emerged in a snarl. "And you came here to get my blessing?"

"No."

"Are you going to marry him?"

Her gut clenched. "I don't know."

She glanced up at his face, afraid of what she'd see there. His eyes black and fierce, his whole face taut. He lifted a brow. "I see. You came here to see if maybe you want me instead."

Susana swallowed but held her tongue.

"Well, you don't. I can't do this any more. There isn't enough of me left to play games. I'm just trying to keep my head above water here..."

"And I sucked you under." The first words she said in a normal voice surprised them both.

"Yes." A hollow laugh shook his muscles. "Yes, you sucked me under and carried me far out to sea on the undertow. I'm just trying to swim my way back, so don't..." His voice cracked, and he looked away to the window.

"You never did tell me what happened to you."

"There's no need for you to know about that. Let's part with some of my dignity still intact."

"No." She shook her head, staring hard into his eyes. "If we part, I want it to be because we stared all the facts in the face and made a decision about the future. Together. No more gazing into crystal balls or cards looking for answers. And no more secrets."

"Bold, aren't you? What makes you think I want you in my future?"

She didn't answer. But she saw something flickering in his eyes. Almost as if a flame had popped to life like the pilot light in her old gas heater.

"Come, Joe." She took his hand, trying to ignore the swirls of energy that stung her fingers as they wrapped around his. And she led him toward the bedroom.

"No," he blew out a snort. "No way. I don't know what you're planning, but we're not..."

"We're not going to do anything but talk. No naked fortune telling today." The cool, almost amused sound of her voice amazed her.

"That's a relief."

"We need somewhere to sit down, and I notice you haven't been spending your time furniture shopping." The only additions to the apartment were piles of papers spread out over the floor.

"I've been busy working."

"Good. How's your business going?" Cool, calm and collected. She sounded like a grown up.

"It's all right. I've got three contracts and hired a couple of software developers. Things are looking good."

"I'm glad to hear that." She sat down on the bed and patted it, inviting him to sit next to her. The conflicted expression on his face revealed his doubts, but he sat anyway.

She shifted herself to the middle of the mattress, crossed her legs and arranged her skirt over them. Joe hesitated, perched on the edge of the mattress.

"Come on, get comfortable."

She watched the muscles bunch below his rolled up shirtsleeves as he clenched his fists. "I can't."

"Don't then. But talk to me."

"Why?"

"It helps. Trust me, it's my business. My real business. People think they want to see into the future, but that's not important. What is important is to make sense of what you've been through so you don't make the same mistakes again. Have you ever talked to anyone about it?"

"Nope." He looked almost surprised by the realization. She knew from her work that people rarely spoke about the stuff that was eating them alive. Just kept it all buried inside them like a tumor.

"How long were you married?"

"Eight years."

"That's a long time. And were you ever happy?"

"Sure. I was gone a lot, though. At sea." He rubbed his temple. "I guess that helped. We were never really together all the time until I left the Navy. And by then I'd let her down. I let everybody down." His fingers moved to the scar at his waist, rubbing the raised line of pale tissue.

"And one day I came home from work and found her in bed with another man." He closed his eyes and clenched his fists. "I want a divorce, she said. Right there in front of him. And he was my business partner. An old Navy buddy I'd trusted and loved like a brother. *I want a divorce.* I'll never forget those words as long as I live. Our marriage had been struggling, we both knew it wasn't perfect, but marriage is a commitment." He turned to Susana, eyes hollow with pain. "You know? A lifetime commitment. You have trouble, and you work through it together. It's something you can count on..."

His fists clenched and unclenched as he stared at them. Then he shook his head slowly. "But you can't count on anything. I learned that the hard way."

She wanted to touch him, but she knew better. She didn't dare offer more half-hearted comfort that could only hurt him more. He needed someone who could give him their whole heart. Their whole life.

She wanted him to be loved. *Ain't that cute, Susana.* Maybe you can get married to Frankie and set about finding a loving wife to look after Joe. A practical arrangement for all concerned.

The thought of another woman in Joe's arms stole her breath and made her muscles seize. She could handle hearing about his ex-wife, because that was over and done with. But the future?

The future. Always there like an apparition, hovering just out of reach. She'd tried to see into it and ended up right here in the present—with Joe. Was this where she was meant to be?

Joe lowered himself slowly back down to the mattress. "You know, it does feel good to talk about it." He turned his head to her. "You're not as crazy as you look."

"I look crazy?"

"You look like you've stepped out of a Dickens novel with your long skirt and blouse, today even more so with that scarf over your hair. I think it's cute."

Her hands flew to her hair and pulled out the scarf.

She'd forgotten all about it. It was part of the "gypsy fortune-teller" costume Granna had favored, and it did keep her hair out of her eyes. She clutched the piece of colorful fabric between her palms, which were starting to sweat.

"Don't be embarrassed." A smile crept across his mouth. "It's good to be different."

"I've been different all my life, and it's getting old." She twisted the scarf in her fingers.

"We're all getting old, but with age comes wisdom."

"Does it? Sometimes it feels like it's the other way around."

"Ain't that the truth?" He turned onto his side, facing her. Sudden energy roared between them, and a surge of anticipation heated her blood. But he rolled back and snapped his glance up to the ceiling. She struggled to keep her breathing silent.

Joe's shirt had fallen to either side of his chest, revealing the tattooed eagle, which shifted as he took a deep breath. "When you're young, you don't have any idea of the many ways you can screw up your life. Ignorance is bliss."

"I don't know much about ignorant bliss. Too much rigid tradition and too many bitter old women in my upbringing."

"I think we enjoyed a little ignorant bliss together." He inclined his head slightly and smiled. Her heart squeezed.

"Tell me about the scar." She nodded toward the white curving line that slashed across his belly.

"She's so romantic," he said to the ceiling. A smile tugged at her lips. "You try to tell her you..."

What?

"Oh, never mind. I'll tell you about my scar. My

scars." He lifted an arm from behind his head and ran a finger over the scar on his face. "I'm not as pretty as I used to be."

Susana had a flash of memory of Joe as she'd first seen him ten years ago. She suppressed a laugh because he had been pretty. Big brown eyes, clear shiny skin, features so breathtakingly handsome it had made her all hot under her preteen collar. And best of all he'd been totally unaware of his own appeal.

"It was an explosion." He sat up like a shot. "Oh, shit. I can't sit while I talk about this." He stood, and started pacing about the bedroom. "I've talked about this before. *A lot*." He glanced at her. "I had to, there were a lot of legal hearings. I narrowly escaped getting a dishonorable discharge."

Her face must have betrayed some surprise because he nodded. "Yup, ugly as all get out. You'll see me in a different light after I tell you the story of my scars. But I'll tell you."

He turned and continued pacing. "We were patrolling waters off South America, keeping an eye out for drug traffic. I was in naval security, not the computer kind at that time, the 'always carry a weapon,' kind. We heard there was a boat with suspicious cargo and I was ordered to board it and investigate.

"I'll be honest and tell you that kind of thing scared the hell out of me. I don't think too many'll tell you different. But I got in the dinghy and went over with..." He paused and drew in a slow breath. "With Jamie Andrews, a good friend."

He'd stopped pacing and stared hard at the blank wall. Susana couldn't see the ugly images in his mind, but his agonized expression played out their reflection. She realized she was digging her nails into her palms, and she tried to unclench her fists and breathe.

"I was about to board when I got a radio call that there were hostages on board. A woman and three children, who'd been snatched at the port. I was ordered to retreat. But I could hear the children screaming..."

He swallowed hard. "They were speaking Spanish, which I knew from my Dad..." He wiped a wrist across his face, which was sweating. "Screaming–'save us!' and I... I knew I'd been ordered to turn back, but I couldn't just leave them..."

He turned and strode in the other direction. "Jamie tried to convince me to retreat to our boat, but I *ordered* him to come with me... I was his superior..." He glanced at Susana, pinning her with a fierce stare. "He came."

He turned and walked along the wall furthest from her. "There was all kinds of screaming and yelling when we got on board. I didn't think about anything but getting those kids off the boat. It was a small boat and they were all cowering under a table in the galley downstairs. Jamie held a gun on two men while I grabbed two of the children, both girls, about six years old, and told the mother to bring the third, a toddler. We scrambled up on deck and the mother was just climbing into the dinghy with the youngest child when..." He sucked in a harsh breath and his shoulders heaved. Then he turned and stared at her.

"I don't know what happened next. I woke up in hospital. Someone fired, I don't know if it was Jamie or one of the kidnappers, but the whole boat blew. The fuel tank ignited." He paused and Susana held her breath.

"Jamie died, and the kidnappers. The two children I was carrying drowned when the blast blew me overboard and knocked me unconscious. I'd worn a floatation device so I was rescued and stitched up and lived to tell the tale to a court martial hearing."

His pacing slowed and he turned to look at her. The regret etched on his face made her heart ache.

"I'm so sorry, Joe. You were doing what you thought was best."

"The mother and her youngest child lived. That's what got me off the hook, that I'd saved them. I was in jail, for chrissakes." He looked at her, his eyes hollow with pain. "I always prided myself so much on being a good Navy man, but in one split second I made the wrong decision and five lives were snuffed out. I can't ever forgive myself, and the Navy wasn't too keen to forgive me either. My career was over after that, as well it should be."

He looked at her, his hands hanging by his sides, "I don't deserve to be alive. And frankly, I've wished I wasn't."

"You tried to save the children."

"I disobeyed a direct order. I trusted my gut. And got seventy-eight stitches in it as a reward. See what happens when I follow my instincts?"

Susana climbed off the bed. Pins and needles pricked her flesh as she moved slowly toward Joe. "You trusted your gut when you kissed me. And I trusted mine when I invited you back to my apartment, even though we'd just met." She stood in front of him, absorbing the heat and tension coming off his body in waves.

"See what a mistake you made?" His low voice echoed around her, and he looked right into her eyes, defying her to disagree.

"I don't think it was a mistake." She held his gaze, while her heart thumped painfully against her ribs. "You're a good man, Joe."

"Yeah, a good man responsible for the death of two

innocent children and a close friend. And two total strangers who should have had a fair trial, no matter what they did."

"We all make mistakes."

"A cliché, but true. And you made one the day you took me in and got me all stirred up about you. Now your cousins know you've been a bad girl, and others will find out too if you don't stay away. Don't mess up your life, Susana. There's no going back. I learned that the hard way."

Her fingers itched to touch him, to absorb some of the pain she could see tormenting him. Every muscle in him was tight. She wanted to release the tension and let him rest. To make everything better. She'd promised she could lift a curse on him but that was just talk. Talk was her only true magic and she knew words had the power to heal, but right now her well was dry.

She didn't know what to say so she said the first thing that came to mind. "I love you, Joe."

The muscle ticked in his cheek. "I think you said that before, and you still kicked me out. Love doesn't count for too much in the real world."

"Maybe it could." She licked her dry lips as a whole host of frightening possibilities crowded her mind. Marriage to Joe and exile from her family. Marriage to Frankie and a lifetime without Joe. No matter how she looked at it things weren't pretty or easy or...

Joe looked right at her, his eyes black and unreadable. "You already made your choice. You know what you need. You'll build a career for yourself, and you'll have your family. It's a good choice, a practical choice. No one can have everything."

"But you're my destiny, Joe." The words rose to her lips along with sudden conviction that they were true.

She spoke them very deliberately, meaning every word. "You're my fate. The reason I never married." Her palms were hot and she wiped them on her skirt. "I'm meant to be with you. We're meant to be together. It's my destiny, as a woman... As a Rom woman."

"You told me Rom couldn't marry outsiders. Your family will throw you out. That's the end of being Rom for you."

"No. I'll be Rom until I die." She paused. They still hadn't touched, but energy buzzed and hummed between them.

Until Joe came along she'd been drifting along on a predetermined course. She'd made choices based on what she knew others wanted for her. But Joe had showed her she could make her own choices. Just as she'd chosen to ignore her vision of the two of them back when she was young, now she could choose to seize that future with both hands.

"I don't want any other man but you, Joe."

"You hardly know me."

"I know you as if we were born together. You're in my soul and I'm in yours. I wouldn't be a good gypsy if I turned away from my true destiny." A smile pushed its way to her lips. Suddenly everything seemed so simple and obvious she couldn't imagine why she'd fought so hard against her fate.

"But I'm damaged goods, Susana. You can do better."

"You're seasoned, matured..."

A hollow laugh rocked him, "Weathered, like a tough piece of wood."

His mocking analogy broadened her smile. "You've acquired some checks and cracks, the way any broad beam will, but you're solid. I'd stake my life on you. And

I'd like to, if you'll give me the chance."

Joe blew out a blast of air. Susana held her breath. She'd asked him to spend his life with her. And now she wanted that future with all the power she possessed.

"You gave me hope, Susana." He looked at her steadily. His face bore no expression, but his eyes burned through her, heating her blood and quickening her pulse.

"And then I took it away." Cold seized her fingers and toes. She'd betrayed him once, betrayed herself. Could he trust her now? "I promise you on my life I'll never do that again."

"You'd have to give up so much, and I have to give up nothing. It doesn't seem fair."

"Ah, but you're wrong. You have to give up your anger, your sorrow. You'd have to trust in me."

"I trust your word." His voice was gruff.

"You shouldn't. Words are just noise. Trust my body."

Her fingers shook as she unbuttoned the front of her blouse and parted it. She heard Joe's breath hitch. She unbuttoned the back of her skirt and let it fall to the floor. Her blouse slid over her shoulders and joined it. Awkwardly she climbed out of her underwear until she was stark naked. The room blazed dark orange in the fading sunset.

"I give you my flesh, my heart." She'd kept her eyes lowered, but as she looked up they locked onto Joe's. "To be yours for the rest of my life."

She heard a strange sound in Joe's throat. He blinked, his eyes blazing.

She took a step forward. Her skin tingled, stirred by his body heat. She raised her hand and pushed his shirt back over his left shoulder. He shrugged it off and pushed down his jeans until they both stood naked, bathed in amber by the last rays of the setting sun.

Joe stood with his hands by his sides, coiled strength waiting. "You've breathed life back into me, Susana. I was dead inside, like a statue..." He paused, staring at her, his eyes suddenly soft, lively, shining with new hope.

"And now you can feel again."

He nodded and raised a hand to cup her cheek. And the sweet sensation of his skin touching hers sent a ripple of almost agonizing pleasure shivering to her toes.

"I trust you, Susana. You've never lied to me."

"I'll never lie to you. I'll never cheat on you." She spoke with assurance born of total confidence in her own loyalty.

"I know. You're like me, I can see that now. When you pledge yourself, it's for life. No matter what."

She nodded, her heart so filled with love for him that it squeezed painfully.

He lifted his other hand until he cupped her face in his palms, the heat from his hands scorching cheeks that blazed hot with emotion.

"I love you, Susana. Will you be my wife?"

"Yes," she whispered. "I'll be your wife. From now on we'll live the same life, share the same destiny. Make our own family." She looked into his eyes, meeting the intensity of his gaze, and matching it. "My troubles will be your troubles and your troubles will be mine."

A sweeter burden she couldn't imagine.

He took her hand tight in his, and for a moment she felt the lines on their palms—head, heart, fate—shift and adapt to each other, their lives taking the same path.

She stepped forward and Joe's arms wrapped around her shoulders, hugging her tight. His chest heaved as emotion racked his strong body. "I pledge myself to you,

Susana." His breath was hot on her ear. "I'll love you and cherish you and take care of you until the end of my life."

She believed him with every atom of her being. "I know you will, Joe. And I promise the same to you. We've waited a long time for each other, and we deserve to love each other for a long time."

"Is that a prediction?"

She leaned close, so she could whisper in his ear. Her heart swelled with joy as she held him tight. "It's a promise."

THE END

Jennifer Lewis is the bestselling author of more than twenty books. She has lived on both sides of the Atlantic and been addicted to books since she learned to read at age three. Her stories have been translated into—at last count—twenty-two languages and are read on every continent, except maybe Antarctica. She lives in South Florida with her family, and when she isn't writing she's usually kayaking.

www.jenlewis.com

www.ingramcontent.com/pod-product-compliance
Lightning Source LLC
Chambersburg PA
CBHW022112170626
46808CB00002B/708